ALPHA'S ENEMY

BEARS OF THE WILD

LOLA GABRIEL

Alpha's Enemy

Text Copyright © 2019 by Lola Gabriel

All rights reserved. This book or any portion thereof may not be reproduced or used in any manner whatsoever without the express written permission of the publisher except for the use of brief quotations in a book review.

This book is a work of fiction. Names, characters, places and incidents are either the product of the author's imagination or are used fictionally. Any resemblance to actual persons, living or dead, or to actual events or locales is entirely coincidental.

First printing, 2019

Publisher

Secret Woods Books
secretwoodsbooks@gmail.com
www.SecretWoodsBooks.com

SECRET WOODS BOOKS

Receive a FREE paranormal romance eBook by visiting our website and signing up for our mailing list:

SecretWoodsBooks.com

By signing up for our mailing list, you'll receive a FREE paranormal romance eBook. The newsletter will also provide information on upcoming books and special offers.

1

AXEL

Axel drained his beer and brought the bottle down onto the bar top hard enough for the tall, brown-haired bartender to turn around at the sound. He raised his eyebrows, put down the glass he was polishing, and bent down to open one of the fridges.

"These helping?" he asked, putting a fresh beer in front of his only customer.

"Not really," Axel said. He was leaning on the bar, shredding a coaster. His blue eyes were already slightly unfocused. "Get me a chaser? And drink with me?"

The bartender sighed. "Axel, it's the afternoon."

"Come on, Byron, I'm heartbroken over here." Axel took a swig of his beer, and the bartender, Byron, placed one shot glass and then another on the bar.

"She wasn't right for you, and you knew that from the beginning. We were in here fifteen years ago, and you were *um*-ing and *ahh*-ing about whether or not you two should get serious. I don't want to pull the older and wiser card, Axel, but I told you; when you know, you know. And you do, you know."

"Yeah? I think you just pulled it." The two men threw back

their whiskeys almost simultaneously, and Axel gave his lips an exaggerated smack. "Another one, my wise old friend?" he asked. Then, he continued his thought, "Okay, sure, but we were together for a while... and she slept with that—"

"No more liquor." Byron cleared the glasses away. "I'm at work, and you're a mess. Beer only. And do we have to keep digging through the details of what she did? You know she's paying for it. She won't be able to show her face here for decades, if ever. What's she going to do? Marry him?"

Axel cracked a smile for a second, and his face became boyish and charming. But it really was only for a second. Then he hung his head and went back to his half-destroyed coaster. Byron shook his head and returned to polishing glasses.

"If I didn't know how hurt you are by all this, I'd say you're milking it, Axel. You know you look good as the brooding anti-hero. You're aware that there's no one but me here to see it, right?"

Axel sighed. He was painfully aware of the empty bar, of the fact that there was still light out, at a time of year when the sun set at two.

"Maybe I'm practicing," he said, "for when I feel ready to get back on the horse. My tale of woe will have women clamoring for me." He straightened up a little and ran a hand through his mess of dark hair, sweeping it away from his face. He knew, realistically, that no one wanted to see him looking this down. It wasn't vanity; more like a need to keep up appearances. There were certain things that were expected of him.

"Sure," Byron said, "because you need the help." Again, Axel flashed his dental-commercial smile for half a second.

"Okay, okay. But it's not just— I'm not just angry. I miss her, or who I thought she was... I don't like being at the house because it's half empty, and what is there reminds me of her.

Why do we even start relationships, they always end up like this. With pain."

Now Byron smiled. "Nice dramatic monologue," he said and got out another beer. He walked around the bar as he twisted the top off the bottle and pulled a stool up next to Axel's. "Today, we drink away your pain. Tomorrow, back to real life. Okay?"

Axel held up his beer. "To drinking things away!" he said.

Byron lifted his bottle, but he held it back from Axel's instead of clinking it. He barely looked older than Axel. There was some gray creeping into his brown hair, but only enough to add a slight air of distinction. Even though he was perhaps holding slightly more weight than was optimal, he was still a strong young man. A little tired, perhaps, though that could be because he had a family and ran a bar and... Well, he was Axel's go-to, which Axel supposed hadn't been easy lately.

Finally, Byron came up with a toast. "To the next one being your mate, and for there being no pain!" Clink.

After his long sip, Axel raised his eyebrows. "Right, sure, but there's always pain. Either you break up or one of you dies."

Byron rolled his eyes. "Jesus, Axel. We're drinking pain *away,* not trying to stimulate it. Let's play darts. And don't stab yourself with them."

At that exact moment, the bell announcing a new customer let out a trill. Both men's eyes moved to the door and the woman pushing it open.

She was petite and blonde, wrapped up against the cold of the Fairbanks fall in a long down coat. She had a couple of bags with her, and she was having trouble with the door, trying to push it open with a hip. Axel made a move to get up and help her, but she made it inside before he could. She was flushed with the chill. She looked up and smiled at the men sitting at the bar, her green eyes crinkling at the edges.

"Thanks for the help, lads. Just a cold and helpless little

lady trying to make my way through the snow." But she was happy to be in the warm, it seemed, as she put her bags down and stamped a light dusting of snow from her boots. Taking off her gloves, the woman walked toward the bar. "How do I get a drink in this place?" she asked, gesturing to the lack of obvious staff.

Byron's stool scraped against the wooden floor as he pushed it back to stand. Rather than heading round to his post behind the bar, though, he planted his feet firmly and crossed his arms.

"You don't," he said. "You aren't drinking here."

The blonde looked taken aback. She raised her eyebrows and continued unzipping her long coat. "I'm in a bar, aren't I? I'm not hallucinating? Where's the owner?"

Still in his tough-man pose, laughable to Axel, who knew his oldest friend's soft nature, Byron said, "I'm the owner. And I'm telling you, this isn't the bar for you. In fact, we're closing."

"What kind of a watering hole closes at one in the afternoon? The sun's not even down yet," the woman argued, beginning to pull her zipper back up. "I think you've got a faulty business model." At this, Axel laughed. He put a hand on Byron's plaid-shirt-clad shoulder.

"Out of attack mode, big man. Can't you tell she's one of us?" He shot her a look. "It's practically radiating off her." The blonde shot him a look back. And it was skeptical.

"I can go and spend my money elsewhere," she said, "if you boys want to fight or fuck or... whatever it is you need privacy for."

"And she's funny!" Axel said.

Byron shot Axel a look now, a look that said, *This is not what you need right now*. But the customer is always right. Especially if the customer is Axel Lingdson and the establishment is based in Fairbanks, Alaska. Finally, Byron relaxed.

"Fine," he said, "the stranger can stay. But my eye's on her.

Alpha's Enemy

And," he added, "on you." He strolled around the bar slowly, dragging it out. Axel shook his head.

"Sorry about my friend," he said. "He can be overprotective, but he makes a mean cocktail."

"What if I want a beer?" The blonde went back to taking off her outdoor clothes, slipping off her coat and sitting down. She was curvier than she had looked in the coat, despite being small. Her sweater was tight, and she was wearing black jeans tucked into her boots. Axel tried not to look her up and down—obviously, knew he shouldn't—but he was already long past tipsy.

"He's also great at opening bottles," he went on. The woman turned pointedly toward the bar, hiding herself somewhat. A sullen Byron grabbed a lager. He opened it with unnecessary flourish and set it in front of her. Axel thought he was holding himself back from a sarcastic curtsy.

"Put it on my tab," Axel said.

"Right. Your tab..." Byron turned around, engrossing himself forcefully in cleaning and restocking, both of which he'd already done that morning. Axel had one hand on his beer and had turned to face the prickly blonde.

"I'm Axel," he introduced himself, "and you—"

She turned her head, resting those sharp, green eyes on him. "I know who you are."

Axel was taken aback by her delivery. Of course she did. Every shifter in the state knew who the pack leaders were.

"You've heard good things?" God, what was he doing? A twenty-year relationship really erodes your flirtation skills. And it wasn't like it had been his longest, either. How had he done this before?

The blonde ignored him, turning back to her beer and pulling out her phone. Byron glanced at the iPhone and began scrubbing his countertop harder. Technology was a touchy subject for him; the bar owner was never quick to adapt. He'd still been jumping at the sound of a home phone ringing when cell phones came in. This would only compound his distrust of the newcomer, Axel thought, though, really, the technology thing was a Byron problem and had nothing to do with anyone else.

"So, why are you in town?" Axel tried and almost visibly cringed. Was it the lack of practice, or the alcohol? The woman turned to him again, and she pushed her long wavy hair back behind her shoulders.

"Alone time," she answered, but she didn't take her eyes off him. He stared right back, and he didn't know why. He couldn't stop looking at her heart-shaped face and those eyes. She looked away. "Get me a whiskey," she said to Byron, "a double." He poured her a cruelly short shot. Then he glanced at Axel and grudgingly topped it up. "Look," the woman told Byron, "I promise I'm not here to cause trouble. Can we declare a truce?"

Axel said, "He's stubborn, you'll have to try harder."

Not even turning her head, the blonde added, "I'm not here to be hit on by sleazy alphas, either. You're the same in every damn pack."

Behind the bar, Byron snorted with laughter. Axel shot him a look. "Oh, you're on her side now?"

Byron shrugged, keeping at his work. It was by no means the evening yet, but outside the bar's window, Main Street was darkening. Fall in Fairbanks, and every day was shorter than the last.

Customers were beginning to trickle into Byron's bar, filling the seats around Axel and the stranger. Axel got a few pats on the back, and a couple of people asked how he was doing. More bought him drinks. Beside him, the beautiful stranger had her elbows on the bar and her blonde hair tucked behind her ears. After a while, she pulled out a book. Axel kept stealing glances at her, even as he talked to various friends. He could feel the fuzz

Alpha's Enemy

of real drunkenness coming upon him, lapping at him like warm water.

Things he could say to her... ask about her book. The author's name looked Russian, and it was a hefty volume. She was deep into it, concentrating. She must have brains as well as beauty. But Axel already knew she did. She was sharp. Funny. And he couldn't ask her about her book! Classic sleaze move, asking a girl in a bar about what she was reading. And she'd called him a sleaze. *Him*. He should tell her he was better than that—tell her about Leonida.

Yeah, because that was better: blather about his ex to a new woman. Vaguely, Axel wondered who she'd been referring to when she'd said all alphas were the same. Then he remembered he and Byron had never played their game of darts. He should challenge her! Darts were darts. Not sleazy and not wholesome, just... throwing sharp stuff at a board.

When Axel leaned toward her, the blonde put a finger in her book to hold her place. "Darts?"

She raised her eyebrows. "Excuse me?"

"Would you like to play a game of darts?" Axel really hoped he wasn't blushing. Or slurring.

"Are we putting money on it?" The blonde smiled. "Because right now, I like my odds."

"Sure," Axel said, "but I'm pretty good..."

The woman folded down the corner of the page she was on and closed her book.

2

KEIRA

Keira adjusted the fly on her dart and shifted her feet. Axel hadn't been lying; he was good at this game. But so was she. Her dart landed true, double bullseye.

"Beginner's luck," Axel called behind her, but he was grinning. He'd switched to water after they'd made their wager. Not that it would help much at this point.

The bar was now loud enough that he and Keira had to shout to hear one another. Mostly, this had kept their competitive banter to a minimum. The occasional heckle.

As Axel stepped up to grab the darts, Keira said, "You're not used to losing, are you?" Axel missed the board and then hit a twelve. He'd already closed twelve.

"God damn it!" he cursed.

And she'd just been beginning to like him, Keira thought. All that anger wasn't unexpected. He reminded her of every alpha she knew. But he'd been up to joke earlier, and his smile—well, his smile was what let him get away with it, she supposed. She held out her hand flat for the darts. Axel put them in her palm, his eyes searching her face. His fingers brushed the sensitive skin of her hand. They both flinched a little. That had been intense.

After quickly stepping back, Axel said, "You know, I'm not some meathead, power hungry—"

"Right," Keira cut him off. "You're going to cry when you lose, are you?"

Axel shook his head. "You threw me off—"

Keira was already stepping away from him. She didn't hear the rest. She threw a dud, and it was her turn to curse, though she was much bluer than Axel. Why was he getting to her? She was here for a reason. She should stick to it.

"I'm going to get a drink," she said, walking past Axel and slamming the darts down on the table beside him.

"You trying to catch up with me?" he called. But she had reverted to her early tactic of shooting back cold glances. Her hair whipped over her shoulder as she turned to deliver one, and she almost walked into someone.

"Oh, shit, I'm sorry," she apologized, looking up at the tank of a man she had almost bounced off. Her eyes finding his face, she looked quickly down at the floorboards. "My bad," she finished and continued quickly toward the bar. There was no way he would recognize her. Her uncles hadn't traded with him for over a hundred years. She'd looked different then, in a bonnet and furs.

Reaching the bar, she glanced back. The large, bearded man was looking at Axel. But then, most of the bar was glancing occasionally over to Axel. Checking on his demeanor, she assumed, wondering whether or not to be worried. Axel looked tired, more than anything. Well, a little drunk, and very tired. He glanced down at the darts as if he was counting them, and then he rolled them back and forth across the table.

"Two beers," Keira said without thinking. Byron slammed them in front of her so that they both foamed. When she got back to the table, she shoved one of the beers toward Axel. "Don't get any ideas," she told him. "You bought me one earlier. Now we're even."

Axel smiled that smile again and put the beer to his lips. Unusually full for a man's, and not chapped by the quickly advancing cold.

"I don't even know your name," he said.

"Right," Keira replied, "and that's not how you ask someone their name. You think this is a rom-com?" She grabbed the darts. Lining up to aim, her hand was shaking a little. She glanced back at Axel. He looked a little stunned. "And that's a win!" she announced, clearing the short expanse of sticky carpet between herself and the chalkboard and crossing, then circling the final number on her side. She turned back to Axel. "So, check or cash?"

Axel was seated at the table, drinking the beer she'd bought. "Honestly, I didn't think I was going to lose. I don't have cash."

Keira nodded to the windows, where snow was beginning to blow in the orange light of the streetlight. The flakes were small and hard looking. Visibly crystals. They would scratch your face like tiny pieces of glass.

"I don't think so," Axel said. "Take it in drinks. Put them on my tab. You don't even have to talk to me."

Keira leaned against the table. He was rubbing the condensation off his beer bottle with a finger in circles. His hair was in front of his face. She wanted to reach out and push it back.

"I'm just here as a stop on a trip," she said. "I can drink with you for a little while. But I want my money's worth. Get me a martini."

~

WHEN AXEL SET the martini glass in front of her, he looked from it to her with almost puppy dog eyes, so startlingly blue and so strangely needy... or innocent? No, there was no way it was that. Needy made more sense. He'd also gotten a martini.

"You like martinis?" Keira asked, and he shrugged. Then he shook his head.

"No, not really. But they've gone in and out of fashion. And I didn't want Byron to think I was pandering to you... though I guess he knows what I drink..." She was sat down now, aware of herself leaning a little toward him over the table and trying not to.

"Right?" Keira straightened her back, pulling all her hair behind her shoulders with one hand. "Sometimes I wake up and don't know what year it is. Then my phone goes off and I'm jolted into this decade." Axel unleashed his smile, and he leaned back in his chair.

"Right. Well, things move so quickly. One little thing happens, and your whole life is in a tailspin. Believe me, I know that feeling." He took a sip of his beer. He looked down at his lap like maybe it had been the drink giving him loose lips. He rubbed his pretty blue eyes.

"When did you start this afternoon?" Keira asked.

"It was barely afternoon," he said. "Midday." She had a hand on her bottle and one on her own thigh, as nonchalant as she could manage.

"What do you mean?" she asked. "What's happened?"

"You care now? I'm not a sleaze?" She sighed, leaning her chin on the heel of her hand.

"I don't know you. You might be. But you seem tired and sad." At this, Axel's eyes flicked up to meet hers, and they were full of that vulnerability again.

"I'm not," he said. "I'm not a sleaze. Or whatever. I just got out of something big. I don't remember how to do this."

Keira leaned forward, not at all unaware of what she was doing. "Do what?"

"Flirt, or whatever," Axel answered. She was almost sure she detected the slightest of blushes, although he was snow-pale and the lights of the nearby TV were washing his face. She leaned back and smiled at him.

"Yeah, you're doing a terrible job. You're lucky I don't know anyone in town, or I'd be long gone."

His eyelashes were curled and thick. He blinked at her, and she didn't know if it was the drink or him, but she was feeling something. He ran his hand through his wild dark hair again, pushing it back so ineffectively.

3

AXEL

"Look," Axel said. "I promise, I've just got out of a long relationship. We lived together. My house is half empty. I've no idea how to be single, how to do any of this crap." Again, he was worried color was heading to his cheeks. He drained his beer. "My ex— We were together over fifteen years. More like twenty, if you count all the on again, off again. I know, not the longest relationship ever, but we lived together, and I loved her, and..."

The blonde was gazing at him with her beautiful green eyes. Looking right at him, like she was seeing him, not thinking about something else. He wasn't sure he could remember the last time Leonida had done that, but how was that a surprise?

"She just left me," he finished. "It was rough." The woman seemed to soften a little, her petite features becoming gentle.

"Okay," she said. "I'm sorry. It happens. You want me to buy your drinks?" Axel tried to smile, but despite the woman in front of him—her wit, her darts skills, her eyes—he was thinking of Leonida leaving.

"I might need you to, if I'm honest. The mission today was to drown sorrows, and I can't get past mildly drunk," he said. "I'm sorry about earlier. I didn't mean to be creepy and crass. I'm out of practice. I mean. I'm normally good at— Not that I ever did it all the time. Or, not since I was basically a cub— Damn it."

The blonde was smiling. She laughed a little. "It's not at you, it's with you. Or, it's both. I think you're drunker than you realize. And you're sweet. Surprisingly so."

Now Axel knew he must be blushing. He looked down at the sticky table top.

"Not always," he said. "At least, not everyone thinks so..." Then he looked up at her again and did his best to smile genuinely. "Okay," he began, "so where did you come from?"

She paused for a moment. "I was in Paxon."

Axel made a face of surprise mid-drink. "Paxon? What were you doing there?"

"I have an uncle there," the woman replied with a shrug. "I spent some time visiting. We're all over the state, you know." Axel waved a hand in the air as he took a drink.

"Yeah, yeah," he said. "We inhabit the wilderness, where we escaped to, blah, blah. But really, *Paxon*? There are what, forty residents?"

"Forty-three at the last census. But no one's moving there, and there aren't many young people. The whole state's changing."

Axel cocked his beer bottle toward her. "Life is change," he said.

"Uh-huh. Like your girlfriend leaving you?" the woman prodded. "Having fun accepting that?" Then she scrunched up her face. She was pretty even like that. "Shit, sorry," she mumbled. "That was harsh. I get loose lipped after a few drinks."

"Not loose lipped enough to tell me your name, though?" said Axel. She was chewing a fingernail. Again, still cute.

"Hmmm," she hummed. "No, I think it's part of the fun now. Part of the mystery."

"So you're having fun?" Axel asked, leaning toward her slightly.

"It's not the worst day I've ever had."

Their eyes met. He wasn't sure if either of them had intended it. A few seconds passed. A smile was playing at the edges of the woman's lips. Her eyelashes were long, he noticed. It gave her light eyes a darker look. Sultry, maybe, though he didn't know when he might have used that word last.

"She cheated on me," he muttered. Then he wondered why he'd said it. But the woman didn't look away.

"I'm sorry. That must have been hard."

It was like Axel wanted her to know everything about him. All his darkest secrets, his most questionable thoughts, and all the best of him, too. Whatever that might be.

"Yeah," he said. "With a human." The mysterious blonde— that was what she was now, the mysterious blonde, and she knew it—sucked air in through her teeth.

"Ouch." She reached out and almost touched his hand with hers, but she held back. Her fingers were frozen inches above Axel's, and then she withdrew them. "It doesn't sound like she was right for you. Like she was good enough. I mean... you're sweet. I don't know how she could..." It was her turn to blush. "Do you want to get out of here?"

Axel's mouth was dry. He nodded and drained his beer.

As they walked over to their stuff, Axel could feel the eyes of half the bar on them. He wanted to put his hand on the small of the woman's back or her elbow. Take her hand, even. But he resisted the urge. They both put on their hats and pulled up their hoods.

IN THE SNOW, they walked silently for a few moments. They hadn't agreed on a direction, just turned right and walked. Then Axel reached for her wrist, pulling her close to him. Their breath was rising in white plumes in front of their faces, mingling in the streetlight glow above them.

"Did you feel that, earlier?" he asked. The woman didn't reply, just looked at him. "When we were playing darts... my fingers touched your skin..."

She closed her eyes, as if in pleasure at the memory. She nodded her head. Axel was still holding her wrist. She was pressed hard against him, but there were layers of fabric between them.

"I want to see you," she said. "Please?"

Axel took her ski-gloved hand in his own. They kept their arms pressed together, as if for warmth, although there was no way they could be feeling such a thing through their winter clothes. As quickly as they could, they crunched through the fresh coating of snow, heading for the edge of town, where the houses petered out.

4

KEIRA

When they reached a large gap between houses, they walked into the dark. They would have better vision soon, but for now, they allowed themselves the luxury of a remaining streetlight glimmer. Who was going to argue with Axel if they saw them there?

Without speaking, they both began to strip off their layers, piling them together between their feet. Their coats and scarves and sweaters were tangled in the snow. When Keira got to her t-shirt and the high waisted jeans it was tucked into, she stopped. She unlaced her boots (too expensive to ruin) and stood in the snow in her socks, waiting for Axel to do the same. They backed away from one another. She pushed her hair away from her face. She wanted to see him, even while she shifted herself.

She saw it begin at least. Axel's blue eyes turned gold, and he twisted his neck from one side to the other. Keira felt the change coming for her, too; that feeling like claws grabbing her stomach in the darkness. She hunched over. Her hands hit the snow, and the cold came up into her elbows and then her shoulders like pins and needles. The breath was gone from her for a second and then returned, doubled. Power rippled through her. She walked a few steps, testing the sway of her body.

It didn't hurt after the first couple of times, those agonizing transitions in an already

agonized teenage body. Now, hundreds of years and thousands of transitions later, it felt almost good—like wobbling a tooth, or the ache a day or two after a hard workout.

When she stopped pacing, shaking off the change, Keira knew Axel was behind her. She circled slowly, and at the same moment, he turned to face her. He was a medium-sized bear for a male, yet lithe. His fur was a dark brown, almost black, unusually so, and it was speckled with snow. It looked like the night sky above them. His eyes were the shape they were when he was a man. He walked toward her, and when he was close, he put his snout to hers. He licked at her light-colored fur, brought a paw to her neck, and gently batted her.

It wasn't that Keira usually felt as a bear would feel when she was shifted, but neither did she feel like her human self. Animal took over some of her. Smell and sound and hunting became important. But when Axel's paw hit her fur to ruffle it and a claw brushed against her throat, there was that electricity again. Something she had never felt before tonight, and certainly not in animal form.

Keira pushed back, her paw coming down on Axel's ear, almost succeeding in getting his head to the ground. He licked it. She ran at him, and he ran backward, then in a circle. Then at her, until they were play fighting like cubs, both covered in snow. Then up again, back to starting positions, circling; a dance, one that was normally only ever danced by close friends, family. Eventually, both bears reared onto their hind legs. They were eye to eye. Staring. Panting.

Keira moved forward. Their prints were clear in the snow, declaring their presence. This was happening, being recorded, at least for the next few minutes, even though it shouldn't be. Keira pushed her nose into Axel's shoulder, licking him, biting him just slightly. It was too much for the human in her. She backed away fast enough to kick up snow, which landed all over both of them so that he had to shake his head, surprised and chilled.

They circled one another a few more times before Axel pawed at the snow.

As she returned to human form, Keira gasped. She was on her knees on the ground. It wasn't that she was surprised by the snow—she'd done this plenty of times. She was surprised by everything else she felt. When she could finally lift her eyes to Axel, only a few feet away, she saw that he was as well.

The moment he noticed her watching him, he began crawling to her. He was sweaty from the transformation, his hair hanging over his eyes. He pulled her toward him, on top of him, and the warmth of his body made her shiver. When he kissed her, it was so much more than that feeling of electricity. It was a lightning storm. One of her hands was in the snow, the other at his jaw, lightly stubbled. He smelled and tasted of booze. Keira could feel him hardening against her, and she pushed her body against him. *Yes, please. Do that for me.*

Axel pulled back, and she strained forwards, but he held her face lightly. All his force was in his arm, while his hand caressed her cheek. In the light of the streetlamp, his blue eyes glittered against his dark hair and the white snow.

"You're beautiful," he said, "now and when you're shifted."

Keira laughed. "So are you." Intentionally, she shifted against him. His breathing quickened, and he kissed her again.

"Let's go back to my place?" he asked, though he was pulling her damp, panting body against his. "We'll freeze to death out here like this. No more fur." Her reply was just to kiss him again. He tasted so good. Like whisky, warm against the cold of the air and sweet against the snow's tang. "You're shivering," he said when Keira pulled back.

"So are you," she breathed as she twisted around him to nibble at his ear.

"I'm lying in the snow," Axel laughed. "Of course I'm cold." He put an arm around her, pushed his hips up, and flipped them over. Keira gasped as her thighs, then her butt and back, hit the snowy ground. "See," he said, "it's cold." As he said this, he bent his head down to kiss along her collarbones. She shuddered, and not from the cold, though it was a sharp tingle reaching from her back all through her.

"Take me home," Keira half-moaned, pulling his hair a little.

Axel stood up, pulling her up with him, picking her up briefly before they were both standing. They pulled on their clothes, watching one another. He was pink cheeked, pale. He was slim, but his shoulders were broad and covered with a few scars, probably received in his bear form. He moved fluidly and without thought. This was the best of what shifting meant for them as people: when you came back into your human body, you kept some of the animal grace, some of the ability to feel and not think, at least for a while. It could become almost an addiction.

Keira pulled her t-shirt on, not bothering to tuck it in. As it brushed down over her breasts her desire for Axel reached new heights. She had to step forward in her unlaced boots, pull his face down, and kiss him deeply.

"It's just a few blocks away," Axel mumbled, even as he pulled her back to meet his lips one more time. She wanted him so badly, more than she could remember wanting any other man.

Alpha's Enemy

Coats zipped up, they almost ran, hand in hand, back toward the street. Their fingers were interlaced, no gloves. Keira pulled his hand up to her face and kissed it, and he made a noise like a contented animal. Almost a purr.

It was still snowing, though only lightly. She glanced back over her shoulder; the snow in the field behind them was scuffed from their human bodies rolling in it, but the prints of the dancing bears were all but filled in. It was a shame. She wanted to see their patterns.

Axel led her back toward town, then a left and a right, and he stopped at a small, two-story house. It was cladded with wood and had a deeply sloped roof to deal with the snow. He pushed her gently against the front door as he searched his pocket for his keys, kissing her neck. His big soft hand against her waist was warm as a paw. He was lapping and nipping, and when he finally got the door open, Keira almost fell into the living room, but he swung his arm behind her and caught her. She stumbled backward while he stepped forward and kicked the door closed.

She unzipped his coat, and he swung her around so that he was pulling her toward the staircase in the corner of the room. On the stairs, they fell in a heap, both trying to kick off their boots. Axel's laugh was infectious, and soon they were laughing and kissing in their socked feet. The room was spinning a little. Keira couldn't tell if it was the drink, the sudden warmth after the cold, the tumble to the carpet, or the way he smelled. Damp animal mixing with warm skin, whisky, the scent of herself. They pulled off one another's coats, left them on the stairs. Then his hands were under her untucked shirt, cupping her breasts, his calloused thumbs brushing her nipples. He lifted her top with his teeth, grabbed it with one hand, and pulled it off over her head. She lifted her arms for him, then put her mouth close to his ear.

"I want you inside me so badly."

Axel's breath caught. He dropped her t-shirt, stood, picked her up, and carried her to a room at the top of the stairs. His bed was a queen mattress on the floor. Placing her down on it, he said, "Sorry about my room—" But Keira didn't care at all. She didn't let him finish.

She kissed his stomach as he pulled off his own shirt, and she put both hands on his belt buckle, undoing it. She felt him swelling beneath her, teasing him until she pulled down his boxers, then enjoying his moans as she took him in her mouth, holding the backs of his thighs and taking as much of him into her mouth as she could until he squeaked and groaned and leaned one hand out to support himself against the bedroom wall.

Keira pulled back and looked up at him. Axel was flushed, his hair pushed back from his face and his eyes shining in the half-light of the bedroom. He wriggled out of the jeans he still had half on and lay on top of her. He held her hands down, arms above her head, pinning her to the bed.

"You're perfect," he said, kissing her jawbone, her collarbones, and down her body.

For half a second, she felt a pang of guilt, but there was too much pleasure for that. Too much of a lightning storm, its power collecting just below her bellybutton. As Axel kissed further down her body, his hands slipped from her hands to her wrists to her upper arms to her breasts, where he concentrated his energy for a while before taking one hand to undo her tight jeans. She lifted her hips to let him peel them off her, and he held her like that, with one arm beneath the small of her back as he threw them into a corner and dipped his head between her thighs, letting her hips sink a little as he buried his face in her and used his tongue.

Light danced behind her closed eyes. Keira couldn't help but cursing harder than she had when she'd been playing darts. Never in her two-hundred and ninety years had she come close to these waves of ecstasy which were rippling from Axel's mouth on her. She moaned and pushed herself toward him, taking one of his hands and pulling his face to hers so she could taste herself—taste him and her together.

"Please," she groaned, guiding him into her. "I need you."

"Oh, my God... you feel so good." No guilt this time. Not even for moment. No room now for anything but that electricity, that warmth, Axel's skin sticking to hers as he murmured sweet things in her ear and pushed into her, moved with her, until they were both crying out.

5

AXEL

Axel couldn't sleep. The mysterious blonde was curled against him, breathing sweetly in the dark. Her back and thighs and buttocks were pressed against him, warm and soft. Beneath the comforter, he stroked the curves of her side.

Everything up until their game of darts was something of a blur: her walking into the bar, Byron grandstanding on his behalf... She was so funny; smart. And Byron's toast earlier still, "To the next one being your mate, and for there being no pain!" Axel had said something glib, but what did Byron care? He'd been bonded for centuries. What did Axel's romantic missteps even look like to him?

Axel propped himself up on an elbow to look at the woman. He didn't feel weird, watching her sleep. He was fighting the urge to kiss her. He smoothed her hair back over her shoulder. He didn't want to wake her, but he needed to see her better. Her sweet elven nose, her long eyelashes, the way she was sleeping with her lips turned up into almost a smile. He would never be able to leave this bed, he thought. They would live in this bed now, forever, together. Until they starved to death, he supposed.

Alpha's Enemy 25

He knew he should at least try to get some shut eye, but her pull was tidal. Sleep would mean leaving her until morning.

Axel thought again about the afternoon, and it was only then that Leonida swam back into his mind. Leonida... Axel had been so upset about her earlier. He knew this didn't change things, that he should still at least be angry. He had been disrespected—the whole pack had been disrespected. But what good would anger do?

He lay back down, curling himself around the sleeping body next to him. He fit like a puzzle piece. He had been ruined, he knew, since the moment his fingers brushed her palm when he'd handed over the darts. That electricity. Their charges meeting and combining. And now it was a warm buzz, an afterglow. Her breathing synced up with his, as well as her heartbeat under the arm he had wrapped around her front.

Axel wondered what the bartender would think, if he would be cocky about his stupid toast. He hadn't made it happen, of course not. He'd just gotten lucky. Not as lucky as Axel, though; no one in the world could be feeling as lucky as Axel did as he drifted off to sleep.

6

KEIRA

When she woke up, Keira rolled onto her back, rubbed her eyes, and reached a hand out for Axel. When she didn't feel his body next to hers, she was disappointed for a second, and then her stomach dropped. What the hell had she done?

She pulled the thick white comforter up over her head and groaned. Limply, she punched the mattress beside her with the back of her fist. This was not a part of the plan. She rolled over, trying to wrap herself up completely, shut out the morning. His pillow smelled like him. God, it smelled good. Why did he smell like woodsmoke? Keira let herself indulge, her face half buried in the scent of him, but only for a moment. It was almost enough to have her calling out for him to come back to bed.

She sat upright, determined to make better decisions today. Was this a decision, though? It wasn't up to her, or either of them. It was chemical, animal. She groaned again and laid the back of her head against the wall. She could smell coffee being made downstairs. Her jeans were balled up in the corner of the room, and they'd knocked a load of books and papers over. She crawled around, still slightly wrapped in the covers, but she couldn't find her t-shirt. Once she'd pulled on her underwear, she grudgingly grabbed Axel's from the night before. He would want her out of it once he'd heard what she had to tell him, and not in a good way.

Keira stood up and had to lean against the doorframe. They'd definitely been drinking, but that wasn't a good excuse. Nothing was. Even when she felt it, she should have been honest. This was no way to start the rest of their lives. At the top of the stairs, she paused. They were strewn with coats and boots. She remembered Axel's hands cupping her breasts, the way he had taken her shirt in his teeth. It should be around here somewhere. She had to hold onto the bannister, her legs a little wobbly at the memory.

There were noises of drawers opening and closing from the kitchen. Was Axel... humming? Was he going to make this harder for her by being adorable? Well, it was her own damn fault. In the hallway, Keira turned to look for her t-shirt amongst the mess, but when she did, there he was. He stood in the doorway to the kitchen, smiling at her. He had bed hair, and his smile reached his eyes in a way it hadn't the day before. He was shirtless, barefoot, and holding a spatula.

"Good morning," he said, and he loped lazily toward her until he was at the stairs, where he scooped her up toward him from behind and kissed her. Keira melted into him for just a moment, and then she wriggled free.

"Wait," she said, walking forwards so that he was forced back toward the kitchen. He stepped back fully onto the linoleum. It must be late; the sun was coming through the windows. On the little kitchen table, there was a pot of coffee and two mugs, and he had been in the middle of making eggs. The countertop was a mess. Axel put the spatula down.

"What's wrong?" he asked. He looked a little afraid, his brow tense. Keira walked over to the frying pan of eggs and pulled it from the burner, turning the stovetop off. He reached out for her hand, and the side of his fingers brushed hers. She jumped back as if she'd been burned.

"No," she said, "you can't touch me while I tell you this, or I won't be able to... It's too much." For a moment, there was relief on Axel's boyish, beautiful face.

"You still feel it, right? I'm not crazy?"

"No," Keira answered. "I mean, yes. I mean, you aren't crazy, I feel it. We're supposed to be together... mates... but we can't be."

7

AXEL

Axel began to laugh but stopped when he saw that she was tearing up, about to cry.

"What do you mean? You're scared? So am I! We've never done this before."

She was shaking her head. "No, you... you're going to hate me..."

Standing in his kitchen, bathed in the weak midday light, she looked impossibly beautiful. Even almost crying. He wanted to wrap his arms around her and never let her out of his sight again. That, however, was when it struck him, almost at the same moment the words came out of her mouth. He didn't know who this woman was.

"I didn't tell you my name because I thought you might know it," she said, her voice cracking a little. "I said I came from Paxon, and I did, but usually... before that... I'm from Juneau, I'm —" She could hardly talk through her sobs, and Axel couldn't take it. He pulled her toward him, holding her to his bare chest so that her tears rolled down his stomach.

"So, our packs don't get along?" he asked and kissed the top of her head. "This is stronger than that, we can work it out." She pushed firmly away from him, took a step back, and wiped her eyes.

"I made this mess, let me finish," she said. Her voice was no longer shaking or cracking. "I'm Keira. We met when we were children." Axel felt his face start losing what little color it had. He knew what she was about to say, and he wanted to freeze time to stop her saying it. He wanted to tell her to stop there, they would run away together, but it couldn't leave her lips.

Of course, it did.

"Chance is my brother."

AXEL WALKED PAST KEIRA, sat on a chair, and began pouring himself a coffee. He needed control of something, maybe. A coffee pot would have to do. It was a good twenty seconds before Keira walked slowly around the table and pulled out the chair opposite.

"What are you doing?" she asked as she sat.

"Drinking coffee," Axel said, his face expressionless. There should be a storm raging inside him, but it was all silent. He was in the eye. "Why are you really in Fairbanks?" he demanded, trying not to meet her eyes and failing. Still damp with tears, they were the green of dewy grass. He wanted to reach across the table for her.

"He... he asked me to come," Keira answered. "I didn't really want to. I really was in Paxon. We have family in the area, the middle of nowhere. Axel, I'm so sorry. I was sent to find out more about Leonida, if you might know where she is. My brother is thinking about allowing her into Juneau."

Axel's hands were in his hair. The anger that had disappeared in the night was back with full force. He closed his eyes to feel it, because when he looked at Keira, it became blunted, quiet. "Was any of this real?"

Alpha's Enemy

Keira jumped out of her chair. Her hands were on his shoulders, then her arms wrapped around him, and her lips came down to his ear.

"Of course," she told him, "of course, how could I fake this? I've never felt anything like the pull I do for you. From the first moment we touched. You know that."

Axel knew he should wriggle free of her, but he couldn't. She was making him weak.

"What have you told him?" he asked. "Have you told him about this?"

Her laugh tickled the side of his face. "No! When would I have? I just woke up."

"You just came downstairs!"

"I just woke up! You know I did."

Axel opened his eyes. Her hair was brushing his face. He could smell her shampoo, and under it, her, and under that, the tiniest hint of her bear scent. He took her right arm and pulled her around to face him, pulled her onto his lap on the chair. Keira's face of surprise almost made him smile, and when he bent to kiss her, he forgot everything. Her legs were bare, and she was wearing his shirt. He tugged on it to tell her to shift further up him, closer to him. He knew she would be able to feel his excitement beneath her, and that it would undermine any anger he mustered. But he didn't care. His thumb traced her bottom ribs, the lower edges of her breast as he held her waist beneath the shirt.

Keira was the one to pull away.

"No," she said, "we have to try to think clearly." But even as she said this, she was caressing his neck, pushing her face into his naked chest. "I want you so badly," she murmured, almost as if she expected him not to hear. At least that was one question answered. This was real, and it was happening. Her hands were in his hair, tugging gently.

"Keira," Axel said, "we shouldn't—" But he didn't make any move to stop her.

"You're right," Keira agreed, jumping off him. "No touching. We can't think when we're touching." She looked down at herself. I'm going to put clothes on." She pulled off the shirt she was wearing. Her exposed breasts looked wonderful and full in the light. Axel almost took a step toward her. Then he stopped himself and caught his shirt as she threw it at him. He bit his bottom lip.

"Ugh, Keira..." He pulled his shirt on. It smelled like her. Just what he needed. He should be so angry at her. When he thought of Chance, the idea of him taking in Leonida, his blood boiled. But Keira... She calmed him. How could he feel this for Chance's sister?

Their families had been enemies for a generation. Their fathers had begun it with some feud that neither of them would speak of. Neither explained it to their children. It was just there. And now Chance was trying to ramp things up again. It was just like the Juneau pack to do something like this. Chance's father had stolen land from Axel's father, messed with trading deals with human partners back when those connections were important. And Axel's father never *started* anything, but he couldn't let the Fairbanks pack be trampled over like that...

Axel suddenly realized he had a dishrag in his two hands. He was twisting it tight, like he was wringing a neck.

When Keira walked back into the room, she was fully dressed. This didn't make Axel want her any less. He crossed his arms, as if to protect himself.

"So, what will you tell him?" he asked. "What will you tell him about Leonida?"

Keira leaned against the wall furthest from him. "Do we have to talk about her?"

Alpha's Enemy

"You came into my territory to seduce information about my ex out of me!" Axel almost yelled this. "Sorry."

Keira tugged on the hem of her shirt as though she was uncomfortable, trying to disappear behind it. "I wasn't trying to seduce information out of you..."

"Oh, right, sure, come into a bar all dressed up and sit down next to me."

She scoffed. "All dressed up? Axel, I was wearing a parka, and I'd been traveling all day."

Axel shrugged and threw the dishcloth down. "Well, you looked good. I noticed you. I was supposed to—"

"I was wearing snow boots and jeans, Ax. I wasn't intending to be noticed."

"I would notice you anywhere." He took a step toward her, but she put a hand on his chest.

"Ah, ah, no touching."

"You're touching me," he argued.

"Only to stop you touching me!" Axel lingered for a moment before stepping back, leaning against the countertop again. He smiled.

"Did you just give me a little nickname?"

"Maybe." Keira raised her eyebrows at him briefly. "Do you like it?"

"You could call me anything under the sun and I'd like it. Damn it, are we flirting again?"

Keira nodded. "Absolutely."

"Well. Stop it." She opened her mouth to protest, but Axel carried on. "What was your plan, then?" She shrugged, shaking her head.

"I don't know. Ask around a little. Not try very hard. Tell my brother I couldn't find anything out. That Fairbanks is suspicious of strangers. I mean, I wanted to meet you... find out who Chance's arch nemesis is and what's so awful about you."

Axel let out a noise that sounded a lot like, *Humph.*

"Honestly, I hoped you would be awful. And you did a good job of convincing me with the moody face you had on you when I arrived at the bar."

Axel turned so that his back was to her, his hands resting on the countertop. On the stove behind him, the eggs were cold.

"Well I wasn't in the best place. She slept with a human, and not just one. Betrayed the whole damn pack. Betrayed me. She's gone, and I don't know where, so there's your damn information. Run along and take it back to your precious brother. Maybe he'll find her, maybe the two of you will be friends. You have something in common, at least."

He knew he'd turned around on purpose to avoid looking at Keira as he said this. But he stayed like that, his shoulders tensed.

"Ax..." Keira sounded sad, half defeated. "I know you don't mean that. And I'm not telling him anything. Or, I'm not telling him anything about her. About Leonida."

There was a long pause. Axel didn't turn around, and Keira didn't go to him. Finally, Axel said, "You're going back?"

"Turn around," Keira said. Pleaded, even. "Axel, look at me." He didn't, and she stepped forward to take him by the arm. He shook her off hard enough that her knuckles whacked the chair beside her.

"Oh, shit—" Axel turned now. "Are you okay, did I hurt you?" Keira was rubbing her left hand.

"Of course not. I'm fine." She flexed her fingers to show him. "You're not *that* strong, Ax." She put out her hand, cupped his chin, and turned him to face her. "You know I have to go back to Juneau, right? At least for now... while we work this out. Chance has to know sometime. About us. I need to tell him I love you, and he needs to accept it. We can say that, right? We're mates, I'm sure of it."

Axel nodded. Just seeing her hopeful face filled him with calm, with warmth.

"I love you, too," he said. "But apparently your brother is trying to destroy me. And my pack would fall on any member of yours that they knew was in town. Why did you even come? It's so dangerous. Weren't you scared?"

"Yes." Keira shrugged. "But I've had no contact with Fairbanks since I was a small child, so what were the chances? And then there was you, and I wasn't scared of anything anymore."

8
KEIRA

Axel leaned in to kiss her. His stubble was rough today, scratching her chin, but she didn't care. She put her arms around the back of his neck, telling him she wanted the kiss to be a long one; long and slow.

Did he know, as he slipped his hands around her hips, his fingers pushing into the small of her back and drawing her body close to his, that they might not see one another again? At least, for a very long time? His probing tongue, the way he stroked up and down her side and buried his face in her hair after they had pulled away from the kiss, said he did.

"Stay," Axel half-growled. "Or we can run away. Who else do we need?"

Keira's heart leapt at this idea. She leaned back and ran her thumb along his cheekbone. "I want that so badly. But you know Chance would come looking for me. And it's not about what *you* need, it's about your pack needing you. You've known that from the moment you were chosen. You'd resent me. We'd resent one another."

Axel sighed. "You really have to tell him?"

Keira nodded. "I'll leave today," she said. "And I'll be back as soon as I can be." For a moment, she curled herself into him, her head nestling on his chest. He kissed her head.

"The eggs are cold," he said.

"It doesn't matter." She stood up straight and smiled. "You make toast, and I'll heat up the coffee."

THEY SAT across from one another to eat their cold eggs. The sun behind Axel lit him from behind, his mess of hair becoming a halo.

"Do you do crosswords?" he asked. There was a pile of newspapers on the table. This was, Keira thought, adorable. A dorky alpha...

"Uhm... I mean, now and then. I have the NYTimes app." Axel looked comically aghast.

"No way! It's not the same." When she raised an eyebrow, he added, "What? I'm three hundred years old, I can't hang onto a few traditions? Come over here." Keira stood up, and Axel pulled her down onto his lap. "Wrap-around garment for old Roman..." Axel traced the clue lightly with a pencil. "Four across."

"Toga, obviously!" Keira took the pencil and wrote it in. "See?" Axel kissed her shoulder. She leaned closer to him. Even that gave her butterflies. She turned her attention back to the crossword and began writing down from the 'T' of 'Toga.'

"Woah, woah! Across first and then down, you animal." Keira laughed, pointing to the corresponding clue.

"A public house, particularly in the old west," she said. "It's tavern, so I'm putting it in."

Axel let her finish writing, then kissed her shoulder again.

"See, I knew you were clever. You were too mean and funny not to be, yesterday, when you arrived."

Keira turned to face him. Her heart was filling and growing and breaking all at the same time. "And you're not a sleaze. You are the sweetest man. I want to do crosswords with you every day."

Axel kissed her lightly. "We'll do that, I promise. It just... might take a while for Chance to accept this. And, I can be a sleaze. Probably."

She stroked his stubbled chin, which made him look less boyish than he had the day before. He looked in his late twenties with this five-o'clock shadow and furrowed brow, like a man who could lead. "Ax, I don't think we can expect any kind of acceptance. If I try to leave, to come back here, he will come after me."

"I know," Axel said.

"And he'll do what he can to hurt you. I mean that in every way. From finding Leonida and welcoming her to Juneau, to coming here and facing you. I'll try not to let him hurt you, but..."

"Keira, I can handle myself. Just tell him as soon as possible, okay? Because I need you back here with me. Already, it's going to feel wrong without you. Tell him, and then get back here? Whatever he says, can you promise me that? And if I don't see you in a few days, I'll come there. I'll come and get you."

"I don't need rescuing, but thanks for the offer." Keira wasn't fond of the grandstanding. It reminded her of Chance. And if the two of them did end up in the same place, she knew there would be trouble. If she wanted Axel safe, she should just walk away, tell her brother some bullshit story about Leonida, and get on with her life. Shouldn't knowing he was safe be enough? Him knowing she was safe?

As if he'd read her mind, Axel said, "I know you don't. You're one of the strongest women— Sorry, that was dumb, you're one of the strongest people I've ever met. I know that after one night and day, from darts, drinking, talking, and you tricking me into not even knowing your name. Then, fighting in the snow and making love. And now that I've had you... now that I know this feeling, know you, I won't be living if you aren't by my side."

Tears were threatening to fall from Keira's eyes. She kissed him, hard. She twisted around and swung a leg over him so that she was straddling him and they were face to face. She dropped the pencil on the kitchen floor, and it rolled under the table. She mumbled between kisses.

"I need to feel your skin against mine before I go." Axel tugged her shirt off her, then his lips were on her breasts, brushing lightly. "That feels good, Ax," she moaned.

Axel stood and carried her to the living room, her legs around his waist. He laid her gently on the sofa, but she flipped over on top of him and began removing his shirt, then undoing his belt. She leaned down and kissed his neck.

"I'm scared," she whispered in his ear. "I'm scared for you." He pulled her mouth to his, kissing her aggressively. Keira tasted blood and didn't know which of them it belonged to, but she didn't care. "But it's for us, right? It's for this."

"Maybe I should come back with you?" he suggested, but she pulled off his jeans and her own, stroked the hair from his forehead so she could look into his eyes. Axel let out something like a little squeak, trying to hold back his desire. Keira could see the want in him, though, and feel it below her. As she slipped him inside her, all the electric storm energy from the night before hit her at once, and she gasped, arched her back, moaned his name.

Axel guided her with his hands on her hips. She wanted to freeze time. She wanted to stay in this perfect moment forever, but soon, he was gasping and moaning, too. Then they had somehow rolled over and were on the floor, giggling, still connected, and he was holding her hands down again, playing with her while he was inside her. Her elbows were being burnt by the carpet, but she didn't care. She felt so fully exposed to him, laid out like this, and it felt perfect.

Axel slowed down and kissed her neck, then came close to her and pushed himself in deep, again and again. It almost really was like time had stopped, like they would be there surrounded by their protective bubble of pleasure forever, until finally, Keira's legs shook, and Axel shook and groaned, and they were spent.

They lay on the rug in front of the sofa for a long time. Silent. It was long past dark when Keira rolled over, kissed Axel, and raised herself on an elbow.

"There'll be a flight at five," she said.

"You're going today?"

"Ax, I have to. You know I do." She got up onto her knees and stretched. He was looking at her, at her body, as she did so, but she had never felt more comfortable with someone watching her. "The sooner I leave, the sooner I can come back."

Still lying down, Axel picked at the rug. "Or not come back. What if he locks you away?"

Keira laughed. "I'm not a fairytale princess."

"I just have a bad feeling." Alex sat up as Keira gathered her clothes, pulling them on.

"Of course you do. This is a mess... I don't know what Chance will do, Axel. My brother can be unpredictable—" Axel interrupted her with a quiet scoff. "Okay, my brother can be many things. I don't think he'll be throwing us any kind of a party. I may be banished, or—"

"Or I may get a summons?" Keira nodded. This was what had been hanging in the air all day: a summons, a battle, some-thing not seen by an Alaskan pack for a generation. Winner takes all. It was how they used to solve disputes, gain territory.

Alpha's Enemy 41

Keira hoped against hope that she would be able to persuade her brother out of it, but he was fiery. And there was no one Chance hated more than Axel and the Fairbanks pack.

"Let me drive you to the airport?"

Keira shook her head, and Axel didn't argue.

9

KEIRA

Keira had seen her brother angry plenty of times, but never like this. Chance was pacing the room, his thick arms crossed, his face tight. Occasionally, he would mumble, "You're so stupid," or something similar. "Keira, you're so fucking stupid."

Keira was sitting on the sofa, looking out the window more than at Chance. She was waiting for him to calm down, though she had already been waiting a while. The siblings were in their parents' old house, which Chance, of course, had claimed for himself when he became alpha. The floorboards creaked at every one of his angry steps, and the sound was starting to irritate Keira badly, adding to the tumult inside her.

"Chance, he's my mate. He just is. What am I supposed to do about that? I only get one. You want me to live without him?"

Chance turned to her. He was tapping his foot. He shook his big blond head. "You're so emotional, Keira. I shouldn't have trusted you to do anything for me."

"Jesus, Chance, I'm not a child! I didn't want to participate in your idiotic little feud in the first place." Keira leaned back on the sofa. Her brother was the most stubborn person she knew,

Alpha's Enemy 43

and she was settling in for a long argument. She was surprised when Chance stepped forward, grabbed her shoulder, and tried to pull her up off the sofa.

"You're calling him and telling him it's over. You're doing it now, and you're doing it in front of me, and then you're unpacking and staying in the spare room until I can trust you again." Keira recoiled. She held onto the arm of the sofa.

"What the hell?" she yelled. "Get off me! Are you insane?"

"It's not my little feud. It was passed down to me, to us. This is about respect. History. This is about living the way we're supposed to live! Bonding yourself to a Fairbankser..." To Keira's utter disgust, Chance spat on the floor. Even he looked a little surprised afterwards, but he carried on. "I mean it, Keira." He tried to grab her again.

"Chance, you aren't my father. And even if you were, I'm two hundred and ninety years old." She was still wriggling out of his grasp, using her hand to try to get his strong fingers off of her.

"No," Chance said, finally letting go and stepping back, "but I am your alpha. And I forbid you from seeing him again. You're not going back to Fairbanks, and there's no way in hell he's coming here."

Keira also stood up. She didn't want to be near him. Honestly, he was scaring her a little. He was just her big brother, right? Surely, he wouldn't actually hurt her. She was telling herself this, but she was checking she had a clear path to the door at the same time.

"He's using you, you know?" Chance said. "To get to me. Did you tell him? Did you tell him I sent you?" Keira nodded. Was Chance just trying to unsettle her, or did he believe what he was saying?

"Yes, I told him in the morning. We'd already felt it. We spent the night together. Then we had sex on his living room floor. It's nothing to do with you. He hates you, but he loves me. We're in love."

Chance scoffed. "You've known him two days, Keira. Have you spoken to him since? He wants me, not you. This is pretty much a declaration of war. I mean, what would Dad do in this situation? This calls for a summons. I'm taking it to the council. And then I'm going to kill him."

Again, Keira was taken aback. Chance had a temper. He'd had a temper since they were kids, when he'd lock her in her room because she'd eaten the last of a batch of cookies and push her down the stairs for breaking a wooden toy soldier he loved. But she'd never heard him threaten murder. And it sounded like he meant it.

"Chance, listen to me!" She grabbed at his sleeve, yet she wasn't fast enough to stop him from leaving the room. His face was dark with rage.

Keira followed her brother down the dark wood of the hallway. The house had been built by their grandparents, and it had been added to by every generation since. Chance was the first to live in it alone. It was a family home, and full of history. Chance had turned his childhood bedroom into a workout room and taken over their parents' master suite. When he mentioned the 'spare room,' Keira assumed he meant her own room.

Chance was heading for the kitchen, where there was still an ancient home phone, curly cord and all. It was strange how time passed. It felt like forever ago, because time didn't pass exactly differently for the shifters. At the same time, it felt so recent, because she remembered what had been before. Trumpets and scrolls and pomp and circumstance. But they had a damn phone for this kind of thing. All kept their home phones for it, despite the fact that snow knocked out service a month each year and that shifted, they could run to one another's homes more quickly. Now everyone, except for the oldest and most stubborn, had a smartphone.

And so, Chance lifted the receiver. Again, Keira grabbed him.

"Chance—" She tugged his sleeve, feeling so much like a little sister. "Chance, please, I won't forgive you for this! Chance, for me. For me!"

He looked at her. Their eyes were the same almond shape and color, but his were a darker green, flecked with brown. He was breathing hard, as though he was fighting something.

"I have to," he said. "This is what he would have done."

Unwanted, a few tears leaked from Keira's eyes. "You aren't him, Chance. You decide who to be." Chance shook free.

"I'm the alpha. I'm carrying on for him." He typed in the first number and began putting out the call. It was a summons.

The next part would be old school; it had never changed and could never change. Their fastest would be sent to gather the Fairbanks pack to the battlefield. The Fairbanks pack would have less time to prepare, while Chance and his people would have to decide when to head out into the cold, how to time things. Keira dropped to the floor beside her brother. Chance knelt down, receiver to his ear, and grabbed the phone she was fishing from her pocket. She hadn't had much hope of reaching Axel, anyway. She was going to have to go with her pack and try her best to stop things there.

Keira had never been angrier with her brother than she was right then, but more than anything, to her surprise, she missed Axel. She needed Axel. She had to make sure he was okay. She didn't want either of them hurt, but it wasn't even a contest anymore. She had to find a way to warn Axel, or at least to save him.

10

AXEL

It wasn't like Axel wasn't expecting it. The messenger didn't bother coming to his home, even, just stopped at the edge of the village and scratched at the first door. Byron was four-hundred years old; he knew what it meant. He let the grizzly bear respectfully retreat, then shot out the front door of his house, not bothering to undress, his clothes splitting and ripping and falling from him as he ran on two legs and then four. Or that was how Axel assumed it had gone down, from the way Byron arrived panting huge wet steamy breaths into the icy air as he scratched at Axel's door, the sleeve of a shirt still hanging from him almost comically. In any case, it would have been comical if not for the way Byron was showing teeth.

Axel didn't bother pulling his boots on. Soon, he wouldn't need them.

"Okay?" he asked Byron, a hand in the fur over his heaving shoulder. Byron let out a grunt, an affirmative, and Axel pulled himself up and over the greyish-colored bear. He was soft, not as young as he used to be, but Byron could still run. Before Axel could apologize for using his friend as a vehicle, his breath was ripped from his lungs as Byron bounded toward the church.

Alpha's Enemy

47

They were on the old system here in Fairbanks, the one set up for them generations ago when the witches had helped them relocate to the farthest-flung states. And what witch didn't love an ominous bell tower? Enchanted, obviously, so that the sound traveled. It should be audible to whoever Axel intended, though it could still be covered by other noises or ignored, of course.

Axel was deposited at the bottom of the steps. It was a short tower; the weather would allow nothing else. He took the stairs two at a time, wishing for the boots he'd abandoned in his hall as his feet gathered splinters. He knew the transition would push them out, though. At the top, he grabbed the rope. It was old, wet, and it slipped from his hands a couple of times before he could ring it three times. A pause. Clang, Clang. Another pause. Clang once more. He wondered if the newest shifters understood, those who had passed their fifteenth moon and begun to exist in their other bodies since the last time it had rung like this. He wondered if the older were listening.

It took only moments for the huffs and growls of his packs to begin. And then they began to run, a trip that would take a couple of days—a trip it had been years since they'd taken, those of them who knew the way south along the coast. To the halfway point, between their enemies' home and theirs, knowing the rival pack would be waiting for them.

As he shifted, as he ran, Axel could think only of Keira. In all honesty, he didn't know Chance well; only as a distant enemy. He should have urged her harder to be careful. He should have asked about Chance's temper, their relationship, her safety. Would Chance hurt his sister? Would he banish her or lock her up? Axel realized he had no idea, and he felt a huge guilt and a wash of love and protectiveness, even as his muscles burned and his breath came in gasps and his four paws churned up the snow.

It was just over a two-day journey. At night, the shifters whose wives had strapped them with packs provided clothing for everyone, and they set up camp in the traditional way, lighting fires. They ate jerky and camping food, strangely guilty of the fact that their ancestors would have stayed changed to hunt and forage and become even more spent in the process. Axel could barely say a word, and he was circled around by most of his pack, who knew he would be fighting for all of them tomorrow. They trusted him enough not to ask questions. Only Byron, skinny and brown-haired again, looking in his twenties (as they all did in human form, despite their bear-selves slowly aging), sat down beside him.

"The girl?" he asked. Axel, his hands out toward the fire, nodded.

"How did you—?" Byron slapped him on the back and left his hand there.

"You've been a mess for the last couple of days. And she looks like her father." Byron turned to face him.

"Why didn't you say anything?"

"I was going to. I had my suspicions, and I wanted to be sure, but then I saw you together. The way you looked together and saw one another. The way there was something more there than the usual when you got close. I'm bonded, Axel. I see it. Maria and I, we still have that. And our cubs. And... I think this will turn out because it must. She's for you, and you're for her. Her brother is an obstacle, and I'm sorry this is the only way to overcome it."

11

KEIRA

Keira had to follow her brother.

"No," Chance had said. Then, after the change—which he'd made from fully clothed in some attempt, she thought, to show his masculinity—rather than hide his nakedness from his sister, he'd held her human form down with a paw. He'd done it softly.

Chance had been there the first time she had shifted, just a year after him. It still hurt for him, and he'd turned first, seeing the signs in her: the shivering, the quickened breath, the glances up at the sky.

"It's okay," Chance had said then, and he had removed all his clothes except his underwear, his stocky teenage body shivering in the cold night. "It's okay. It hurts, and then it doesn't. Watch." And he'd turned his back to her and shifted, as slowly and controlled as he knew how to at sixteen. Ten minutes later, as Keira burst through her clothes and cried at that first slow change, he had pawed her and licked her cheeks.

She thought about that as she followed him in secret, trying not to crunch the still-falling snow under her paws. She would be distracted by a smell or a thought of bear-Axel or some ripping anger at Chance. But she tried to keep that human thought, that human memory; that her brother loved her and this was all showboating.

Chance was running. Bounding through the forest as if he was happy, and that made it harder. Was he convincing himself? The trees were spiky and evergreen. Following without whipping them back or impaling herself was close to impossible.

They were faster than bears. Faster than anything, really, but the journey still took two days. As the light faded, the men—because it was still men who went out to provide backup for their alpha—shifted and set up snow-hole camps and fires. Keira didn't dare. She couldn't make the mess and noise of camping and would freeze to death, curled up as a naked human in the snow. It was dangerous to stay bear this long. It clouded you, confused you. You still never forgot, but you changed, gave into the animal desires with more ease. By morning, she had eaten sparse berries from low bushes and a rabbit who was out late in season. Her golden fur was bloodstained, though she had the wherewithal to try to wipe her snout off in the snow.

It wasn't until noon on the second day that they reached the clearing. Keira recognized it, despite all the years that had passed. Her father had brought her here once, on his back, before she had made her first change in her fifteenth year. It had been a brawl then, with Axel's grandfather. Her brother had been drunk in his human form the night before, forbidden from his first summons. He'd never forgiven her, she supposed. Or himself. And she had felt, then and for a long time afterwards, that her father had wanted her to take over. She had known she would be the more balanced leader.

But it couldn't happen, and so it hadn't.

KEIRA WATCHED CHANCE PACING NOW, waiting, when he should be resting. Every muscle in his big bear body was tense. He should camp. He should at least burrow. Normally, she would calm him, talk him down, but she was afraid of what he would do if he knew she was here. She'd come out of the back door and kept behind trees. It was a strange feeling to be afraid of her brother for real, her heart beating hard for another man; another alpha. What did that mean for her loyalties? What would her father—?

What did it matter? She'd found her mate. And if she could cross the wide clearing, she would be able to find him, warn him of her brother's rage, tell him about his anger, his weak spots, exactly when he would give up before it was too much. But with every move Keira made, she risked being heard. In the light of morning, it was a little easier and a little harder. She would be seen easier, her light and distinctive coat amongst the trees, but she could see better, too. She would go back on herself, she decided, and circle the clearing from a distance. The worst part was walking away, afraid a paw would come down on her from behind. But she did it. She made her paws as soft as possible, placing each leg down as though she was trying not to break an egg.

She would never make it at this pace.

When Keira turned her head and could no longer see the movement of the camp setting up flickering through the trees, she began to run. She was a mile or more out from it, which meant several miles around, and she had hunted that rabbit in the early hours. She could have, should have, made up the ground then. But the colors were blurring as she ran now, and the smells were getting stronger. Her sides brushing up against branches sent tingles down her spine, and she could hear the snow falling from the trees. She knew she could make it.

After the camp was out of sight, however, there was no way

to tell where she was. And no scent to follow, even though she searched for Axel's, the only one she really wanted to find. It took the movement of the sun over one quarter of the sky to find some snow that tasted of what she wanted.

Chance had been here, but how far had she wandered? Half a sun. What did half a sun mean? Keira had been shifted for two days. Her brain was swimming. She could think in suns and wants and... She ran in the direction of the scent. It was taking too long, and she knew that, at least. Her snout was scratched by thorns until her eyes watered and tears ran down her fur, leaving dark trails. They froze. She ran. She ran. She ran. They scratched. She ran.

The clearing opened up in front of her. Two bears were circling each other. One was snarling, the other trying to keep eye contact. All Keira could register was that it was too late. The bears were kicking up snow. They butted heads hard. An ear was bitten, but she could barely tell whose it was. And then they stood up on two legs, claws out, and they began to rip, to roar as the snow ran red.

12

AXEL

Axel had rested well. He had eaten. He had prepared as much as was possible. But this was no territorial brawl. They circled and pawed, as they were supposed to, as generations before them had done after every summons, however serious or trivial. But once they reared, somehow at the same time, the whites of their eyes showing, it was completely real.

Chance slashed at Axel's face, and Axel dodged. His wet fur was freezing, and it hit him in the eyes. Axel blinked back tears and ice water, going down to all fours. He backed away for a moment. Chance was the larger bear, but Axel was faster, his muscles twitching visibly under his dark fur. Chance was a lighter color, though not as light as his sister. His gums were drawn back, his slightly yellowed canines showing. He leapt at Axel, who, once more, jumped out of the way. If he could just tire Chance out, he would have a shot. Chance was angry, full of adrenaline, but Axel needed this more. He needed Keira, or he wouldn't really be living his life. Perhaps it would be a good thing if Chance killed him, he thought for a moment. Then he imagined Keira alone, with a brother who had betrayed her, and he took his first real lunge.

It was so sudden that Chance was caught by surprise. Axel's claws made full contact. They dug deep just behind Chance's ear, which was ripped half away from his head before he managed to turn and dig his teeth deep into Axel's front leg. Axel felt tendons snap, and a grey film of pain came down over him as he shook free, limping on three legs backward.

The snow was turning red beneath them, then pink as they kicked it up again. Axel tried to breathe slowly, calmly, trying to slow his heartbeat.

The injury had only made Chance angrier. He snarled and circled. He lunged, a fake out, trying to unsettle Axel. Axel thought of his first fights, mock battles with his father and with Byron. When the teenage, unpredictable Axel had roared and clawed and run at his dad after fakes like that, or after he had scratched Axel or rolled him over in the snow, his father had stopped him with a paw.

"Never be the angrier one, Axel," he would say on their walks home. "Let your opponent see red while you see clearly." It had been hard advice to take then, in tussles with older bears when he had wanted badly to prove himself. But this wasn't about proving himself—this was about Keira. He had to calm himself down.

Axel backed away as far as he could, making Chance move forward, making him follow, use up his energy. Chance leapt at Axel when he was close enough, and Axel rolled, his damaged paw held up, but still hitting the snow so that pain shot into him. It was like it was coming from the earth itself. Chance had his back to Axel now, and Axel took his moment. He reared up. Chance turned. Axel snapped at him, and then they were both on their hind legs. Chance was panting hard. His eyes were narrowed. His breath was coming in great clouds, and Axel

Alpha's Enemy 55

could see his own doing the same. He saw nothing but Chance. And he knew Chance saw nothing but him. All the bears watching were silent. And then, almost simultaneously, jaws open, claws unsheathed, they lunged.

That was when she arrived: a smaller female, a golden bear, and the two males smashed into her instead of into each other. Axel's one good paw got her in the back, he thought, but he couldn't be sure. Both he and Chance were too late to pull back. All three bears fell to the snow. There was noise from the audience, yaps and growls and paws in the snow.

13

KEIRA

Keira woke to Axel and Chance above her, both wrapped in blankets.

"Apply pressure," Chance was saying. "For fuck's sake, are you an idiot? Pressure!"

"Where?" Axel was bloody, his left arm was ripped to pieces, and his right hand was dripping red. That hand was on her. "You tore her to shreds!" Axel cried, pressing down. There were tears in his eyes. Neither of the men had noticed she was awake. She lifted an arm to touch Axel.

"What happened?" she tried to say, but it was a whisper.

"You got in the middle." Chance sounded angry, even though he was shaking, trying to hold one of the blankets she now realized were also covering her against a gash in her side. "This was *you*," he snarled at Axel. Axel, though, was looking down at her.

"I want to kiss you," he said, "but I'm trying to stop the bleeding. I'm so sorry." Upon the snow, Keira shook her head, her already wet hair getting wetter. She was numb from the cold, except for the ache of her wounds. She held Axel's forearm, stroked it with a thumb. She looked into his blue eyes.

"No," she murmured. "I shifted—" She took a breath. "I

Alpha's Enemy 57

shifted days ago. It's a blur... I saw you two, and the blood, and I... I wanted it to stop..."

"Keira," Chance said, "don't try to talk. Just stop. Explain later." Then his eyebrows furrowed. "Did you follow us here? Were you... were you shifted the whole time?"

Keira opened her mouth, and Axel said, "Chance is right! Stay quiet, sweetheart."

Everyone in the clearing had shifted back to their human forms. Some were milling around, agitated, but Byron, as ever, had things under control. His tall figure appeared over Keira, fully clothed, carrying clothes for Chance and Axel, bandages, and more blankets to cover her.

"We'll take her to Ambrosia," he said, dropping the clothes by their sides and shooing them away from her so that he could wrap bandages tight around the wounds on her torso.

"Thank you," she mumbled. Her eyelids were flickering, and she could feel herself drifting off.

"Who is that?" Chance asked, looking around as if he wanted one of his men to come to the rescue, too, though Byron had it as covered as it could be.

"It's Byron," Keira said. "Don't worry, it's Byron."

"Axel, put on those damn clothes," Byron said. "No one wants to see you naked."

"I do." Keira tried to smile or laugh, but it hurt too much.

Byron managed a chuckle. "You were right, Axel. She is funny."

Chance had stepped back a little, had pulled on the thermals and jeans provided for him, and was holding the sweater. He was looking between Axel and his sister. Axel was crying quietly, also pulling on his clothes. Keira was watching them as best as she could, but she knew she was about to pass out. She held out a hand to them both, beckoning them closer. Byron shifted, moving away from his nursing tasks for a moment, and

Chance and Axel knelt on either side of Keira on the bloody snow.

"Look at me," she said, despite the fact that they already were. She could just barely see. "I love you... I love both of you. Please don't kill each other. I'll see you later, okay?"

Everything went dark for her.

14

CHANCE

Keira was being lifted onto a stretcher, wrapped in rough blankets. He wasn't helping, and he didn't know why. He was frozen. She had followed him. She had followed him, and he hadn't even noticed, how had he not noticed?

She had been trying to find Axel; she had been coming for Axel. Chance didn't want to think about what that meant or what he felt about it. He clenched his fists. His head hurt where his ear was torn. The blood on his face was beginning to freeze. He brought his sweater-covered elbow up to rub some of it from his chin.

Axel was over by the stretcher, following it as Keira was carried to the edge of the clearing. He was beside her. She had been looking for him.

Before he knew it, Chance's legs were moving. He was on the dark-haired man and had tackled him to the ground. Axel was already bleeding through his sweater sleeves, and the side of Chance's head was an oozing mess despite his attempt at cleaning it up, but they rolled around in the snow anyway, making yet another patch of pink in the white.

"Why did you want her?" Chance was shouting. "Why did you make me do this?" He lifted a hand to hit Axel, but Axel caught the fist in his good hand, trying to hold his bad arm to his chest. He twisted Chance's arm, but Chance was bigger, stronger, and he resisted. Their hands were locked on the ground.

"I don't know!" Axel screamed. "I didn't!" He tried to draw his injured arm in closer to him and grimaced. "Chance, I didn't look for this! We're mates, you know we—"

They were pulled apart by several sets of hands.

"What are you doing?" and, "Stop it!" came from several mouths. Axel held his left forearm tight with his right hand. Panting, Chance pushed his bloody hair from his face.

"I'm taking her to Ambrosia," he said. "I'm doing it."

From behind him, where Keira had been laid in the cover of the trees, came the rough voice of the tall brown-haired Fairbankser who had bandaged her. "You'll take her together."

Chance turned. "What? What's your name?"

"Your sister told you," Axel said. "That's Byron. And he's trying to save Keira's life, so please show him some respect."

Chance looked at Axel now. He had composed himself, like the tussle in the snow had brought him back into his body. He was still holding his arm, shivering, but his feet were set apart, his jaw tight. Chance had to admit he was good looking: blue eyes, dark hair, slim frame. He could see why his sister liked him. Physically, at least.

"We both want the same thing," Axel said. Then Byron broke in.

"Just put on some layers and bandage yourselves up. You're both a mess. I'm going to find a car. We can't run with her, she'd die." And he turned away, running off into the forest, where he would undoubtedly shift.

"He's going to steal a car," Axel said. Chance couldn't help himself, and a half smile crept onto his face.

Alpha's Enemy   61

"You have a good man there," he conceded. "He's right. I don't like you, and I'm not going to, and I don't want you with my sister. But for now, bandage yourself up and put on some layers. We have to save her." Chance strode toward his side of the clearing, where his men were waiting for him, huddled and worried. They needed him, too, he realized as he neared them. They had followed him with almost no information, and he was about to tell them to head home without him. Again, he lifted his arm to his face and rubbed at the dried blood there.

15

AXEL

Axel pulled on a second sweater and a down jacket, a hat, and one glove. He held the other and turned. "Can someone?"

Turner, a young shifter Axel didn't yet know well, nodded. Silently, he walked over, snow crunching beneath his boots. He took the glove and carefully inched it onto Axel's left hand. There was intense concentration on his face. When he was done, he looked up.

"Are you going with her, sir?" he asked. Axel almost laughed but held back.

"It's Axel," he said, "not sir. And yes, I am, but you'll all be fine. You'll be home and warm soon." Turner shook his head.

"Sorry, Axel," he said. "I mean. She's... your mate? Will she come back to Fairbanks if she—?" Axel nodded.

"This is a lot of questions." Turner looked a little embarrassed.

"Uh... we were..." He gestured back to a group of teenagers in a huddle far into the woods. "We were wondering what it's like, to find your mate, and... Well, that fight was cool. I mean, why do we hate the... the Juneau pack? No one has told us."

Alpha's Enemy 63

Axel once again took his injured arm in his good hand. He looked up at the grey sky, at the trees.

"That *is* a lot of questions," he repeated. "The feud has been handed down. My father passed it on to me, and now it's mine to carry. I trusted— I trust him. And finding your mate is— Well, I don't know much, I just did it. But it feels right. I'm more with her beside me." Axel was afraid he was going to tear up in front of the kid. "Go tell your friends," he said, "if you got anything out of that at all."

Turner swirled immediately and ran-shuffled across the snow to the group of teen-shifters staring at him and at Axel.

Now fully clothed against the weather, Axel turned to Keira. Only her face was visible over the blankets she was wrapped in. She lay on a stretcher of tree branches and another blanket. She was deathly pale. Had it been Axel's claws? What inside her had been punctured? Which wound was bleeding the most?

He moved toward her, almost afraid of touching her now, of making it worse—of hurting her more. Her breath was visibly shallow. The clouds of it above her were nothing but small puffs. Axel bent down to touch her face. He couldn't feel it through his gloves, and he couldn't remove them, so he bent further and kissed her. She was still warm, living. He pressed his forehead to hers. The electricity was there still; lighter, a tickle, a warmth. He kissed her again, his gloves uselessly against her cheek.

Suddenly, Axel became aware he was being watched. He stood up and glanced around him. A few people on his side of the clearing were looking, but their eyes were, mostly, pointedly averted. But then he stared across to the Juneau side: daggers from a sea of hard faces. Chance was looking at him, but looked away when Axel met his gaze. Axel turned away from them, too. His torn-up arm was agony. He couldn't move the fingers in his left hand, or his wrist. He hoped Chance's head hurt, that he'd ripped his ear as hard as he had felt in his paw.

And then, the sound of an engine. It was a pick-up truck with a full cab and snow tires. Byron was driving it down a dirt path that led through the trees, but honestly, he was disregarding the smaller ones, knocking them to the ground. When the scratched and dented truck reached the edge of the clearing, it screeched to a halt, and Byron jumped out while it was still running. Axel spun back around to face his pack.

"Hey, four of you! Get her in the back of the cab!"

Byron nodded at Axel and began to sprint across the bloodied, churned-up clearing. He called to Chance, but the big blond man was already making his way toward the car, Axel, and his unconscious sister. As they reached one another, Byron placed a hand on Chance's shoulder and squeezed. Chance flinched, freezing for a moment. Four of the younger shifters were lifting the makeshift stretcher into the backseat of the cab, with one of them keeping the door open, two gingerly lifting Keira's stretcher, and the fourth hovering in case of any kind of disaster. Axel watched them for a moment, out of fear for Keira, and he felt a new kind of pride. He couldn't deal with these pack feelings now, with the way an alpha should, he supposed, feel. He turned back to Chance and Byron just as they reached him.

"What are we waiting for?" Chance asked, chest puffed and hands on hips as he tried not to seem out of breath. Byron looked at Axel and did the replying.

"Absolutely nothing, my friend. Hop in." Byron gestured to the open front door of the cab, and Chance got in. Byron took the driver's seat, and Axel squeezed behind him and sat in the tiny gap between Keira's head and the window in the back. She was so still, so pale; he had to check. He bent down awkwardly sideways and pressed his cheek to hers. Warm.

"What are you doing, dude?" Chance had craned his neck, and he was looking from the front seat.

"I'm checking on her," Axel said, nodding down at his arm. "I can't take my gloves off." Chance didn't look pleased. Axel bent again and kissed Keira softly on the forehead.

"I should be back there," Chance said. "He can't steady her with only one good arm."

Turning the key in the ignition, Byron scoffed. "Whose fault is that, macho man?"

Axel dropped his bad arm, placed his good hand on Keira's shoulder, and held tight.

"I have her," he said, and the truck began to move.

THE AMBROSIA COVEN was inland about an hour. Luckily, the strongest witches were also the closest. They provided medical care in situations like this, especially for the shifters, and in some situations, the shifters did provide, or had provided protection for Ambrosia and many other covens. The relationship was symbiotic in its way.

Getting out of the forest was rough, since the track was all potholes and rocks under the snow. Axel half laid his body across Keira, his good hand on her thigh, trying to keep himself from agitating her wounds but also trying to keep her steady. From time to time, Chance glanced over at them. Axel, when his head was turned to look out the windscreen and see if they were nearly at the road, caught his eye. Chance was still angry. It was clear in those green eyes, darker than his sister's but a reminder of what Keira's beautiful eyes looked like under her vaguely fluttering lids. Axel began trying to catch his eye so he could see a flicker of Keira in them as he held her softly breathing body with his one good arm.

It was a solid fifteen minutes before they reached the highway, which was, of course, better than a dirt track but still not a well-kept road. The icy winters and few warmer summer months meant expansion and contraction, ice and snow and wind. And in rural Alaska, there was little upkeep. Axel tried to relax, to lift himself from Keira, but every bump sent a spasm of terror through him. He could feel her blood beginning to soak into his coat. When he moved slightly, he stuck to her blankets. The blood, her blood, had made it through bandages and blankets and to the fabric of his coat. He wanted to clutch her hard against him, even if he knew he couldn't because that would only worsen the blood loss.

"What are you looking at?" Chance eventually demanded when Axel's eyes met his for the fourth or fifth time.

"You look like her," Axel said. "A little, at least."

"Yeah," Chance spat back, "she's my sister."

As he was driving, Byron glanced back at Axel, checking on his reaction. Byron nodded ever so slightly. Fine. It was fine. Chance was family now, whether Axel and Byron liked it or not. Byron didn't like it, and Axel could see that, yet he stayed silent, despite his distrust of Chance. After his check, he kept his eyes on the road. Axel appreciated his friend's loyalty; his father's friend, probably the person who, at this point, knew him best in the world. Axel was filled with gratitude for Byron all of a sudden. He was about to thank him, his words as filled up with emotions as he was. Then Byron took a sharp turn onto a small lane. It was barely discernible under the snow that lay over it.

"Jesus," Chance said, "my sister's bleeding out in the back! Can you be careful?"

"I'm saving your sister," Byron practically growled, "can you keep your attitude to yourself?" Chance gave Byron a look, but nothing more. His shoulders were tense, his elbows stiff on the armrests.

They were coming up to a long driveway. There was a rusted iron gate, and the place looked abandoned. Pulling up to it,

Byron hit the horn three times, hard enough that Keira moved her head a little and groaned.

"I sent a message," Byron said. He waited a second. "On my phone." Axel kept a hand on Keira's head, leaned forward, and gently put his other hand on his friend's arm.

"Thank you," he said. "Thanks, Byron."

16

CHANCE

Another place Chance had only been to as a child was the Ambrosia Coven. The gate was rusted, bent iron, an intentional deterrent. The coven took no chances with visitors. Chance had come here with his father when there had been a fight between two members of their pack... about a woman, Chance had thought at the time. His father hadn't said, but the bloody man groaning in the back of the car had been calling some woman's name. Maybe it was his mother's or wife's. Chance had been young. It was long before his first transition.

Byron had honked and was currently waiting. Back in Chance's father's time, he'd sent Chance to wiggle through the gate to save time. The witches would eventually sense them, he had said, so they had to be quick. Chance shook his head free of the memory. They had to be quick now as well.

In seconds, there was a woman at the gate. She had a dark nest of hair, and she was wearing jeans and a black down jacket. She lifted the metal like it was nothing, not even unlocking it, and ushered the truck in. Then she disappeared.

"They like to show off," Byron said, "even in an emergency." At the end of the long, yew-lined driveway, was a sprawling house. As the truck drew up to it, the witch in the jeans reappeared. She yanked open Chance's door before he'd had a chance to.

"Agnes Ambrosia," she said. "Did we meet once before? You were a little cub... Anyway, sorry about the house." She waved a hand at the three-story, many-windowed structure behind her. "We had something much better when we were in the homeland. Stone, you know, what you'd expect for a coven, but this is what we get here."

Chance couldn't say he recognized her. Her recognizing him felt almost intrusive, if he was honest. But he bit his tongue, for his sister, as the odd woman looked beyond him.

"Byron! So good to see you, old chap. I mean, we only ever see you when disaster strikes, these days. You should visit!" Now her eyes were at the back of the cab, on Axel and Keira. Chance turned to look at them. Their faces had a matching pallor.

"Please, Agnes," Axel said.

"Dear boy!" The witch practically pulled Axel out of the car and into a hug. Chance was taken aback by this. Why was the most powerful coven in Alaska on hugging terms with Axel and not him? That didn't matter now. They were here for Keira. He stepped out the car as Byron did the same.

"Don't want to break up this party," Chance said, "but does anyone care about my sister?" Agnes let go of Axel and tutted. She looked to be in her forties but was actually older than any of the shifters.

"Be patient, Chance," she chided. "Your father did always tell me you had a hot head." She walked over to Keira, who remained on her stretcher, still, in the back of the cab. Axel touched Agnes' arm, dropping his own bloody forearm in the process.

"She's my mate," he said. "I need you to fix her."

Chance let out a sarcastic little laugh. "Why did you do this to her, then?"

Axel's eyes flashed with anger, and he stepped toward Chance.

"*You* did this to her," he said. "It was *your* summons. It was both of us out there in the clearing, but it was your summons."

Even though Chance felt this like a punch in the gut, he tried to look nonchalant. He hoped he didn't still have blood on his face. He put one hand on his hip. "You seduced her, Fairbanks. You knew what you were doing. As if you didn't know who she was. You were on the rebound from that woman, what was her name? Leoni—"

Axel took a step toward Chance and then froze.

"Boys," Agnes called them. "Behave, please. For the sake of the poor girl, at least." Axel wriggled, as if trying to free himself. "Bring her in," Agnes told Byron and Chance, and Chance felt a strong need to do as he was ordered. Byron shook his head.

"This is the Ambrosia Coven," he said. "They agree to help us because we used to help them. Now it's less symbiotic... Agnes here is doing us a favor."

Agnes smiled at Byron, almost flirtatiously, as he obediently helped slip his sister out of the car. Axel gasped and went a little limp. Then he stood up straight.

"Let me help." He started toward the stretcher, but Agnes stopped him.

"No, they're fine." She wasn't looking at Axel now, but at Keira. The stretcher was oddly light, Chance thought. "Careful on the steps, boys," Agnes said as the three shifters and the strange witch reached the equally strange house. "They get icy."

THE INSIDE of the house was as odd as the outside, a maze of corridors through which Agnes led them down until they reached an expansive living room.

"Lay her down," she instructed, pointing to a large sofa. They did as they were told. "Would anyone like a refreshment of any kind? We have frogspawn soup and some snakeskin crackling, I think. I'll call the help."

Byron smiled widely, and Chance glanced at Axel. Were they supposed to...? Axel looked as disgusted as Chance knew he must. After a moment, the witch laughed.

"For crying out loud, boys, I'm joking! Gullible for a couple of alphas, aren't you?" She looked at Byron again. "All brawn, no brains, as usual." Then she said, "I'll have something brought in. You'll all need your strength." Finally, Agnes walked over to Keira, who was stirring a little, her hair stuck to her forehead and her cheeks stained with sweat. "This is the emergency, I assume?"

"Yes," Byron said. Then he looked at Axel. "I texted, so it was a brief message."

Chance was becoming increasingly annoyed. What was this woman up to, with her jokes and banter? His sister could be— Time was clearly of the essence.

"Who is she?" Agnes asked, beginning to lift a few of the blankets that wrapped Keira.

"My sister." Chance answered just as Axel said, "My mate." The two men shot looks at one another. Their lips twitched as though they would have liked to snarl, had they been shifted.

"Ah," said Agnes. "I see. I see why you would come to me. Good thinking, Byron."

Chance was boiling with rage, but he was trying to contain it. That scrawny sap had just met his sister. He'd known her for almost three centuries. He'd looked after her his whole life, toughened her up into the strong woman she was now. Maybe he shouldn't have done such a good job; she wouldn't have disobeyed him like that if she wasn't so hot-headed and self-sufficient. Chance clenched a fist and tried not to imagine hitting Axel in his smug face.

Agnes observed the bloody bandages, ran her hand along Keira's side, and then rubbed the blood between two fingers and sniffed it.

"Bear wounds?" she asked, turning to Axel. "What happened?" Axel looked at the ground for a second.

"We were... There was a summons. Chance and I were fighting."

"I didn't mean—" Chance broke in. "She wasn't supposed to come! She followed. She was shifted." Agnes raised her eyebrows.

"She was animal for more than a few hours? For days?" Chance and Axel both nodded. "And you don't know which of you did this?" They both shook their heads and looked at one another. There was more confusion and sadness on Axel's face than anger. Chance hated him for that. Even more. Once more, he bit it back. Agnes sighed. "This is going to be tough," she said. "You'll both have to go."

"Go where?" Chance and Axel both asked, again speaking over one another. Before the witch could answer, there was a knock on the door.

"That will be dinner!" Agnes cried. "Come in!" A young woman slipped through the door carrying a tray. "Thank you, Maxine," the witch said. "Set it down on the table. And could you light a fire?"

Maxine walked across the room, barely glancing at Keira, and put the tray down on the large oak table. Then she went over to the fireplace and murmured a few words, rubbing her palms together. A fire leapt up. These women were, Chance had decided, completely insane.

"Eat." Agnes pointed to the bowls on the table. "You'll need

Alpha's Enemy

73

it. Byron," she said, "help me move her to the bedroom." Both Chance and Axel made as if to move toward Keira, but Agnes stood in their way. "Eat! She needs you to." Byron walked over to the sofa to help her with the stretcher.

Suddenly, Chance realized he didn't have the end of that childhood memory. He didn't remember what had happened to the bloody man in the backseat, if they had come to collect him, or whether he had seen the woman he was calling for again. He wracked his brain, but he just didn't know. He couldn't find it. His stomach flipped. The last thing he wanted to do was eat. Sitting down to the steaming bowls of stew, Axel looked at him.

"It's just chicken, right?" Chance picked up his bread. He shrugged.

"I'd eat whole frogs if it meant saving Keira," he said. He didn't break eye contact with Axel as he dipped his bread and brought it to his mouth. Axel picked up his spoon.

"Right," he said, lifted his spoon to his mouth. He laughed. "Just chicken." Chance's shoulders loosened up a little. "I've heard of the Ambrosia Coven, of course. I know the stories. My father told me to come when the pack was in need. But is Agnes..." Axel looked like he was searching for the correct word. "Is she a bit weird? Even for a witch?"

Finally, Chance laughed, a single 'ha,' which he didn't feel good about. Despite that, he nodded.

"Definitely weird," he said. He paused for a moment. "I've been here once before. With my father, when he led our people. One of them was hurt... badly. I was a small child. I remember him being taken into this house."

Axel was staring at him expectantly, spoon hanging above his bowl. He didn't need to ask the question—Chance knew what it was. And he shrugged.

"I don't remember, man. I wish I did. I've been trying."

17

AXEL

It felt like a lifetime before Agnes came back into the room. The fire was blazing incessantly, crackling cheerfully at the other side of the room, and Chance was sat opposite him, looking like a boxer before a big fight. Axel wanted to say something to calm Keira's brother, but he knew it would make things worse. Chance seemed so lost in his own head.

Axel wanted to ask about Keira, about her childhood; if she'd been an awkward teenager; her first transition. He knew her so deeply and not at all. And if... Well, he needed to know her. Whatever happened, he had to, in every way. This new feeling, this new kind of love, was so intense that he almost couldn't think about it. When he did, when he let his mind focus on his feelings for the woman lying so badly injured in the other room, it was almost like his breath was being ripped from him.

At the same time, though, it gave him a new kind of power, he thought. Loving her,

making love to her. That had lit something inside him. Of course, he had always fought for his pack. He would die for his pack, had vowed as much when he was sworn in as alpha, and he had not stopped for a single moment in the years since, meaning it.

His need to protect Keira was softer. It made him feel quite literally warm, that kin to the electricity of touching her, like he'd been waiting for it. And he had, in a way. The idea of a mate had never meant much in the abstract. He supposed he got it now—or some of it. He wanted to discover the rest.

Axel was biting his lip, and Chance was staring at him, probably wondering what he was thinking. "I need her to be safe," Axel told him. "I need her to be okay. And I know you do, too."

The door creaked open, and both men whipped their heads around to see who it was. Agnes was wearing a long-sleeved shirt now, also black, and her hair was tied back with a rag.

"Byron's watching her," she said. "It's touch and go, but with your help, we can do this. I need both of you. I think I can save her, have her right as rain, in fact."

Chance and Axel glanced at one another.

"What do we need to do?" Chance asked, gruffly.

Agnes untied her wild hair. She pocketed the rag. "I need you to go back in time."

For a moment, Axel thought he had misheard her. He waited a beat, giving his brain time to catch up, parse her sentence properly. Nothing happened.

"What?" Chance said, beating Axel to it. Agnes nodded.

"You heard me," she said. "I need you to go back four hundred years." She looked at Chance. "The secret to the well-being of you sister—" She turned to Axel. "—and your mate lies there."

"How?" Axel let out, although he had felt Agnes hold him still with her will alone and seen the little apprentice witch whisper life into a fire.

Chance looked at him. "She's a witch."

"Thank you, Chance. As blunt as your father was, I see. Yes. A spell, of course."

Axel gestured to his arm. He was about to tell Agnes he was hurt, ask her to look at it before any time travel began, when he realized he hadn't felt it aching and burning since he arrived. He looked at Chance.

"Your ear," he said, and Chance put a hand up to the side of his face, feeling his perfectly intact ear.

"Minor injuries are no problem," Agnes explained. "As soon as you enter our circles of protection, they heal rapidly. Especially you shifters." She glanced sternly at both of them. "Which should show you how serious Keira's injuries are. Many of them are internal. We can't move quickly enough."

"Won't we... mess things up? In the past?" Axel asked

Agnes smiled. "Don't kill anyone or sleep with anyone. Time is a loop. Well, not exactly a loop. It's complicated, but this is how it happens, has happened, and will happen."

Axel nodded, sort of half understanding. Next to him Chance furrowed his brow and did the same. Agnes rummaged in her pocket. First, she pulled out the rag, seemed annoyed by it, and threw it on the sofa. Then she tried another pocket. She drew out a slim scroll, sealed with a crest and tied with red string.

"This will protect you," she told them, "when you're there. Use it only in an emergency. You'll know when." Then the witch gestured for the two men to stand. "Ready?" she asked.

"Wait!" Chance startled. "What are we looking for?" Axel was shocked and a little embarrassed that this question hadn't occurred to him.

"Right," he said, "is it a plant, or a... a crystal? A potion?" Agnes smiled softly, as if she were talking to a child.

"You'll know that, too. I'll bring you back once you have it."

Alpha's Enemy

77

Both men gingerly stood. "Put your coats and gloves on, boys. Just as cold then as now. I'm sending you to the woods."

They did as they were told. Axel felt odd as an alpha, being ordered around. Maybe he and Chance had more in common than he'd thought, at least at that moment. Agnes handed him the scroll. Chance looked a little annoyed.

"His pockets zip. Yours just button," Agnes said. And then, "Stand close together please. Two at once is a little tricky. Don't want anything left behind."

The men glanced at one another and shuffled closer. Then closer still, until their arms were pressed together. Agnes had already begun muttering. She walked around them in a circle, making some intricate movements with her hands.

Just as Axel was beginning to think it wasn't working, that this really was just a mad

woman living out here in her topsy-turvy fairground funhouse, he felt what seemed to be hands on his shoulders. He looked at Chance, as if they might have been his hands, and the last thing he saw before his feet were ripped from beneath him was the whites of Chance's wide eyes as he felt the same thing.

For a few seconds, Axel could see nothing, though he felt like he was being stretched in every direction, including directions he wasn't sure existed. And then, suddenly, there was huge pressure and a bright light, followed by a *thunk*.

He was in a pile of snow and spruce needles, on his back, the wind knocked out of him. Above him, the sky was gray. And if it was late fall, like they'd come from, it must be afternoon. Axel lay still for a good minute or two, waiting for the trees to stop spinning and for the ability to breathe to return to him. There was snow in his boots, he could feel it. Unusual side-effect of time travel, he thought vaguely. He sat up and unlaced his boots, took them off one at a time, and shook out the snow and plant matter. It was only as he was retying them that he remembered who he was and where he was, but most importantly, why he was there. His heart leapt in his chest. He jumped up, boots not even fully tied, and began to run before he almost tripped over a lace and bent to fix his boots again.

Keira. All he could see was Keira bleeding. He wanted to vomit, and he didn't know if it was fear or time travel sickness. But if it wasn't Keira he needed to find, who was it?

Chance! Again, Axel leapt to his feet, this time with his boots fully secured, and looked around him. Nothing. There were no obvious landmarks. How did time travel work? Could Chance arrive slower than him?

"Chance!" Axel called into the forest. "Chance? Are you here?"

18

CHANCE

Chance had snow in his gloves and up his jacket. He got to his knees, feeling as though he might vomit. He sorted the gloves and pulled them quickly back onto his hands. Then he had to put his head between his knees for a few seconds. The world was spinning. He wondered why. He unzipped his coat, shaking out the snow that had collected above the elastic that cinched it.

He heard someone calling his name, distant, a voice that was just a little familiar.

Keira! He remembered Keira. He remembered Axel. He remembered why they were here. He got to his feet as fast as possible.

"Axel!" he called. "Axel!" And he retched, leaning against a tree.

"Follow my voice!" Axel shouted. Chance tried to counter with, "Follow mine," but he was almost sick again when he opened his mouth. "Over here!" Axel yelled. Chance lurched toward it, tree to tree. "This way!" Axel continued. Chance would put money on the idiot jumping up and down and waving his arms as he did it.

"Coming," Chance managed, though he had no idea whether or not it would be audible to Axel.

Axel's tone changed. It sounded relieved. Maybe excited, so Chance assumed he'd heard. He rested for another moment and then got as close to a run as he could. It was more of a stumble.

"I see you!" Axel called.

Chance fell into the snow, face first. It was in his mouth. He let Axel haul him up, though he would much rather have gotten himself up. The thing was, he wasn't sure he would have been able to.

"Jeez, Chance," Axel said, his pale face right up close to Chance's. "Are you okay?" He helped Chance make it to a tree so he could sit and lean against it.

"Dunno," Chance mumbled. Then he leaned to the side and threw up.

"Oh, wow." Axel winced. "Okay, better out than in, I guess. Do you *feel* any better?" Chance nodded.

"I think so." Then he rested his head back against the tree. "Gimme a minute?"

Axel backed off and sat back on his haunches in the snow. Chance's breath was still heaving somewhat from the effort of throwing up. But the world was beginning to still. The tree behind his back felt real and strong. The earth was remaining under him. In fact, his ass was cold from the snow.

"Where are we?" he finally asked Axel, raising his head to look at him.

"I have no idea," Axel replied. "The trees... these spruces... there are a lot around Fairbanks. But it's impossible to tell." Axel took out his phone and waved it. "I'm an idiot," he said, "so I looked at this, but there are no GPS satellites up there. Obviously. Amazing how quickly you get used to something, isn't it?"

"You are an idiot," Chance agreed. He wasn't totally sure he meant it this time. Axel nodded up at the grey sky.

Alpha's Enemy 81

"I think the sun will be going down soon. Should we dig snow holes?" Chance looked around.

"Sure," he said. "I mean, no." They had to find the cure, he recalled, and it clearly wasn't buried in the snow. "No, we have one reason to be here."

Axel stood up. "You know I care about finding the cure just as much as you do, but it's going to get dark. It's going to get colder. It's time travel. Surely, Agnes can bring us back at the right time, whenever we find— Well. Whatever it is we're here for."

That time stuff had hurt Chance's head, and he was certainly in no state to consider it again now. He lay his head against the tree again.

"You're in no state to search for anything right now, Chance," Axel said. "Let me dig us in? Just a few hours of sleep. Until you're settled."

Chance was angry again, though he was still too nauseous to really express it. Why was Axel fine when he wasn't? What was special about Axel? What was better? Then he remembered.

"You still have the scroll?" he asked.

Axel put a hand in his pocket and pulled it out. "Right here."

"Give it to me," Chance demanded and tried to reach out a hand for it. "It's protecting you. I need it. I'm sick."

Axel pulled the scroll closer to him. He looked hard at Chance. "She gave it to me... I felt sick, too. It just passed quicker."

"She gave it to you because of your pockets!" Chance insisted. He hoped that was true, but he didn't believe it. He wanted to be the one trusted with the scroll as much as he wanted to feel better. He managed to hold out a hand. Axel gave him the scroll. He closed his fingers around it, waiting for its powers to take hold.

They both waited, looking at Chance's hand. Nothing

happened. They continued staring. Nothing happened. Then they heard branches snapping. Axel grabbed for the scroll. Chance didn't want to let it go, and he held onto it.

"Zip. Pockets," Axel hissed.

Chance was going to hand it over. He really was. He was just making a point, holding onto it for a second too long—just showing Axel he could. Axel stood, put a hand down to heave Chance up, and held him steady by the elbow. The scroll was still in Chance's hand.

And then the shadows in the trees came fully into view: three bears. Three big grizzlies, loping like they knew they had no need to move fast. For a moment, Chance thought of shifting himself, of fighting, but Agnes had instructed them not to kill anyone. Who knew what would happen if they did? Besides, he was leaning on Axel right now.

The bears' hot breath was in Chance's face in the blink of an eye, as well as in Axel's. They sniffed them, their big wet noses right up against them, their eyes scanning their strange clothing. The paws came down next. One cracked against Chance's temple, ricocheting his head into Axel's and then into the tree behind him.

19

AXEL

He couldn't open his eyes, and he couldn't move. For a little while, Axel thought he might be dead. Then he felt the ropes cutting into him, the cold wind on him. He inched open one eye, and then the other. He squinted at the light: two fires. He was facing a clearing and kind of... high up? Again, he tried to move his arms and legs. Whatever was behind him was scratching him, and the ropes...

Axel looked down with some difficulty. He was wrapped with ropes, pushing his jacket into diamonds, almost cutting off various blood supplies. What the hell had happened? Those bears... If they were shifters, they would have smelled the shifter in him and Chance. Where was Chance? Axel craned to look from side to side, which was difficult given his restraints. There Chance was, trussed up just like him. Axel caught his eye.

He tried to mouth, "What's happening?" but lipreading is hard from the side. Axel tried again, this time whispering, "Have you seen anyone?"

Chance shook his head. His hair was matted at the back where it was in contact with the bark of the spruce he was tied to. Both men were tied with their feet well off the ground.

Axel lay his head against the tree and closed his eyes. He tried to think. All his thoughts at the moment revolved around Keira; her soft skin, the way she had breathed words into his ear; how right it had felt to be near her. How, even when she'd told him who she was, in that awful moment, he had wanted her so very badly. And then... Keira soaked in blood. His claws bloody, and Chance's and—

What would happen, Axel suddenly wondered, if he shifted? Surely the ropes would snap. Would they snap before the tree gave? Would he be impaled? Injured enough to shift right back? Or worse, would he have a severed spine? Who would he be any help to? Once more, he wriggled against the restraints. Axel opened his eyes and turned to Chance.

"Hey." Chance didn't respond. "Hey!" Axel tried again, and finally, Chance turned. "Do we shift?" Axel whispered, loud enough for Chance to hear him. Chance opened his mouth. He shook his head a little, like he didn't know what he was going to say.

Then there was the crunch of boots on the snow. Three pairs of boots—three men.

"Here they are," one of them said. All three were wearing coats of thick animal hide with fur-lined hoods that covered their faces, fully hiding them. Their hands were in their pockets. They stood between the two fires so that the flames danced across them, made them appear inhuman and then human again, made their shadows morph and flicker.

The three men moved to let a fourth through. This man was taller, slim. The fur of his hood was grey; wolf rather than rabbit. There were tassels on the ties to his clothing.

"I wouldn't shift," he said from inside the thick fur hood. "My men chose these trees especially. They'll snap, and they'll rip you in two." Axel thought he recognized the voice, even though that was impossible. He cleared his throat. It was sore.

Alpha's Enemy

"I was wondering," he said, hoarsely. "Hard to see my tree from here."

The man who appeared to be the alpha laughed. "Your tree? Glad you're making yourself at home."

Chance wriggled hard enough that Axel could see him out of the corner of his eye, even looking straight ahead.

"Are you going to let us the hell down?" Chance growled. The alpha laughed.

"And lose my advantage?" he asked. "Why would I do that?"

Chance stopped moving. "We're just here looking for something."

"Something?" asked the alpha. Again, there was a zing of recognition for Axel.

"We don't know what," Chance said, "but it's important. We have to save my sister."

"We're looking for some kind of a cure," Axel added. "Is there a plant? Or, I don't know, some kind of medicine? She's hurt. She got caught up in our battle... it was a summons. She just— She ran into the middle." Axel stopped. "She's my mate. Please. Do you have something?"

The alpha let out a little huff of a laugh and yanked a mitten off, putting his hand into a pouch he had slung around him. He pulled out a slip of parchment, wax seal halved on either end, red string hanging from its middle. "The Ambrosia Coven doesn't have a cure for you? They're the best allies we have. The best for healing an injured pack member, anyway. If they can't help you, no one can."

"Please let us down," Axel said. "We'll explain. This is really painful." The alpha ignored him and ran his finger over the seal.

"I would say you couldn't forge this," he said, "but considering your clothing... How did you make it? What is the fabric?" Chance growled.

"Moisture wicking nylon blend," he snarled through gritted

teeth. The alpha put the parchment back in his pocket. He pulled his mitten back on and pushed back his hood.

Axel did know him, though it had been years since he'd seen him: his paternal grandfather, Ingar.

Axel's fists closed, his nails digging into his palms. Tears prickled at his eyelids. He whispered his grandfather's name, but the tall, slim, bearded man was up close to Chance, investigating his parka. When he was apparently satisfied, he moved onto Axel.

"Ingar?" Axel repeated quietly. His grandfather looked up at him.

"You were sent here?" he asked. "By who? The Northern Territories?" Dramatically, he spat on the snow after naming the pack, which had split into several in Axel and Chance's time. Axel almost laughed.

"No. The Ambrosia Coven." Then something occurred to him. "Do we hate the Northern Territories? What about Juneau?"

Ingar glared at him, his eyes full of suspicion. "What do you know of that spat? Has word traveled? What pack are you really from?"

Axel gestured with his head to Chance. "He's Juneau. I'm Fairbanks."

Ingar laughed. "You think I don't know my own pack? You're a third-rate spy, at best.

First, you're screaming your heads off in the woods, and now you claim to be a member of my own pack?"

"Grandfather," Axel muttered. "Please, just let us down and let us explain? There are four of you and two of us. Tie our hands behind our backs. Just let us sit by the fire?" Ingar stepped back, looking hard at Axel.

"When you say Ambrosia sent you," he said, "what do you mean, exactly?"

Alpha's Enemy

87

Chance, exasperated, answered from the next tree. "Time. Travel. We're from the future, dude."

The three men still placed at equal points between the fires began to laugh. Ingar turned to them. He shushed them, waving a hand at them. They stood up straight and were silent again. Ingar swirled back to Axel.

"Well?" he asked. "Explain."

"Let us down," Chance repeated, "and we will."

"Your friend is rude," Ingar said.

"He's in pain," Axel replied. "Various kinds of pain."

"Who are you?" Ingar asked. "Is that an easier question? Name?"

"Axel Lingdson," Axel said, and he took a deep breath. "Alpha of the Fairbanks pack, initiated June 1980." Then he looked to Chance.

"Chance Harstrom," he said. "Juneau alpha since 1984."

Ingar was shaking, but it could have been from anger. Or it might have been a trick of the firelight. He turned to his men.

"Darion," he said, cold and commanding, "bring me a torch." The middle of the three men, who Axel could only assume were the three bears who had knocked them out so brutally, ran toward one of the fires. He was a little chubby, and he ran with a bounce, so the lit end of the torch coming toward them danced like a bug or a loose spark. Ingar held out his hand covered in its deerskin mitten.

"Thank you," he said, taking the torch. Darion stood for a moment before he scampered back to his two companions. Ingar lifted the torch and took a step toward Axel. It lit up Ingar's face, too, the long nose and the striking blue eyes Axel had inherited. He really didn't want to cry. He really didn't want to whisper, "Grandad," but he mouthed it anyway. Ingar's hard face softened a little.

"You look like him," he said. "You look a lot like him. Is it magic? An enchantment?" Axel shook his head as best he could.

"No," he answered. "No. You are Ingar Lingdson, born somewhere in Northern Europe, though you would never say where. Or you wouldn't know where that was in a modern map. Modern as in about a hundred years in the future when I ask... when I asked you. You remembered some strange dances from your childhood, with the men painting their faces. You came on a boat to the Americas, were in one of the first packs to move north as the center of the continent became crowded. You never spoke much, really. I don't know what to tell you. You would let me sit on your knee sometimes, but not often. Now I think it was probably when you'd had a drink. You would tell me things about leadership that I was too young to understand."

The bonds were really beginning to tug at Axel's skin. Ingar approached him, holding the torch closer.

"Hey, Axel!" Chance cried. "Nylon's pretty flammable!" Ingar looked over at him, annoyed. Axel didn't know whether Chance just wanted attention, but he wasn't wrong.

"It is," he agreed. "Hold it up to my face, not my clothes. Look at me. I'm Olliver's son." Ingar held the torch beside Axel for a long time, his eyes searching Axel's face.

"You look almost as he does now," he mumbled. "Almost exactly. Who's your mother?"

"Uh..." Axel hesitated. "I don't know if I can tell you that. I don't want to change anything." Ingar nodded, his thumb stroking at his beard.

"Good answer," he said, "I shouldn't know."

From the other tree, Chance called out again, "You believe us, then? Can we please come down?"

Ingar looked questioningly at Axel, his face still stern. But Axel's grandfather had always looked stern, always in play. Even his big, grey bear form seemed to somehow have a furrowed brow.

"Keira is his sister and my mate," Axel said. "If you could help us... if you even half believe me... please cut us down, let us sit by the fire?"

"Do you know your grandmother?" Ingar questioned.

Axel didn't say anything, but he knew his eyes were giving him away. He couldn't keep looking at Ingar. The older alpha sighed.

"Right." After a pause, he spoke again. "We stay here, by these fires. If you or your companion try to run off, you're dead. If you start to shift, we'll cut you down before you're halfway through. Do you understand?"

His threatening tone was the same now as it ever would be. Axel couldn't help it. "Yes, Grandfather."

Ingar summoned the three shifters still waiting behind him with a flick of his head in the torchlight.

"Get them down," he ordered. "And don't hurt them too much while you do it." He took long strides toward the slightly closer fire and stood in front of it, his arms crossed. Waiting.

20

CHANCE

The ropes were, at this point, hurting Chance so much that he'd forgotten about feeling sick. Or perhaps he felt better. It was impossible to tell. The discomfort level was too high.

The three shifters standing behind their alpha were mostly wrapped in darkness. He kept trying to squint, to see if he recognized family traits of the Fairbanks pack he knew or of anyone else. There had been mixing.

Mixing. Chance was beginning to regret his haste in calling the summons. He had been so angry. Chance's father, Graeme, has instilled in him the distrust of any Fairbanks shifter. And it had been mostly a cold war; avoidance, but still a lineage of deep distrust.

Maybe he'd been wrong, trying to sneak in a hit with Leonida. He'd never heard anything about her other than a kind of bland distrust. She was the lover of the Fairbanks alpha, so she was respected. No one ever mentioned anything about her character.

Graeme had told Chance—and Keira as well—that every Fairbanks bear was a liar, a sneak. Their morals didn't align.

Alpha's Enemy   91

Chance realized now that this was all he knew of the dispute between the packs, the centuries of bad blood, the skirmishes in the woods that left members of their packs dead or wounded. And now Keira. He was responsible for every member of his pack who was wounded or killed, but he was more responsible for Keira. And this time, quite literally.

Chance's stomach turned over as he remembered the feeling of his claws tearing her flesh. And now he'd let the scroll go, too, the thing that was supposed to protect them here, in a time a hundred years before their first breaths. He should be fixing it. He should be part of the peacemaking conversation, but all he could hear were small floating pieces of dialogue. All he could do was shout responses and try to make his voice vaguely heard.

When the chubby shifter came toward him, Chance tensed, ready to shift even if it meant being impaled, or to kick and punch and, if necessary, bite in his human form. But when the blade of a knife flashed, Chance almost lost it. He prepared for the burn of icy metal through his flesh, but it was the ropes that were slashed. Chance was caught by the surprisingly sturdy little man and pressed to the tree trunk until he was standing on his own two feet.

"Thanks," Chance muttered. The short shifter nodded toward the one Axel seemed to know. A relative, Chance assumed, given what he'd managed to overhear.

"Thank him," he said. "Any other chief, and we would've ripped out your throats hours ago." The tall alpha was sitting by the fire, where it had melted the snow. The shifter shoved Chance in that direction.

"Alright!" Chance cried. "I get it, I'm going. Hands to yourself." The shifter laughed.

"You don't get a say." He pushed Chance again, and it was all Chance could do not to turn around and whack him with a gloved fist. At least his feet felt steady now.

Chance was walking faster than the small shifter behind him, hoping to avoid more provocation, when he felt a hand on his shoulder. He jumped.

"Jesus, Axel," he said as the slighter man pulled Chance toward him. Chance tried to resist, but Axel was rough and surprisingly strong.

"That's my grandfather," Axel hissed in his ear, "Ingar. Let me do the talking? I mean, mostly. I think he believes us." Chance was still holding himself stiffly.

"Does he know what the cure is?" he asked. "We're here for one thing, and it's not family reunions." Axel let out his breath in a hiss between his front teeth.

"I don't know, Chance, I've been busy gaining his trust. Agnes sent us here, though. Here and now. I'm sure this is a part of things, and I'm sure you're needed."

Axel kept up with Chance as they made their way to the fire and let him sit down first. They were all cross-legged in the dirt, but the fires must have been burning a while, because the snow was melted, the ground nearly dry. There was the smell of burning evergreen.

To everyone's surprise, Ingar addressed Chance first. "So, you're here to find a cure? For your sister?"

Something in the authority of the bear, already in his own time older than either Chance or Axel, and leader in a time of far more blood and harsh survival, made Chance deferent.

"Yes, sir," he said. "I— We— Our packs don't get along, mine and Axel's. She wanted us to stop fighting, I suppose. She was stupid—"

"*We* were stupid," Axel broke in. Ingar had his head in his hands. His fur hood pooled behind him, deep and dark.

"My goodness," he moaned. He lifted his head. "Go on?" Chance took a deep breath.

Alpha's Enemy 93

"I called it," he continued, "the summons. I was so angry. I've never been so angry. I thought Axel was trying to get to me."

Again, Ingar sighed, waving the story on.

"It doesn't matter," Axel said. "This conflict has been going on a long time, and we allowed it to continue. It's on both of us. We just need a cure. Please, Ingar, what do you have that we don't? What's your secret? What have we lost? No one is around to tell us anymore."

"Yes," Ingar said, looking up and into the fire, a little absent, as if it had only just occurred to him that if these two were the alphas of Fairbanks and Juneau, he must be gone. "Well, we use the spit of a mother bear and the leaves of the forest to close wounds: nettles, grasses, thorns."

Chance flinched. "You close wounds with thorns?"

Ingar nodded. "I suppose, in your future, you have moved beyond such barbarity?" Chance felt himself warming in the face, though maybe it was just the fire.

"Yes," he confirmed. "I mean, we've learned new methods."

Ingar looked between the two men. "Our best antidote to any kind of strife is the Ambrosia Coven. And they have sent you here."

"So the cure must be here, right?" Axel pressed. Ingar shrugged in response.

"It must be, I suppose." He turned to his men. "Bring us liquor," he called, "and whatever you have in the way of food."

21
___

AXEL

Ingar's men brought a clear, throat-ripping spirit and a cloth bag of jerky. Even Chance, despite his earlier sustained sickness, now seemed hungry. The jerky was spiced and savory, and the alcohol hit hard. Axel watched to check that Ingar was drinking, and he seemed to be. This wasn't a party, nor was it any kind of trick or double cross.

"So." Ingar addressed Axel. "You found your mate? When?" Axel bit his lip. He was worried he was about to sound ridiculous.

"A few days ago... but I know—" To his surprise, Ingar smiled.

"Those first weeks," he said, "they feel like the best thing that will ever happen to you, eh? But they're only the beginning. What does it feel like, Axel?" Axel wasn't sure he wanted to describe the intense pull of Keira to his grandfather—the feel of her warm mouth, the rightness of him inside her, his hands on her. "Not that!" Ingar said, his eyes flashing with a glee Axel had never seen in them. "How are you different? What do you want?"

Axel faltered. Then he said, "There is nothing I want more than for her to be okay." He paused. "And I want time with her. I

Alpha's Enemy   95

want calm. I want, more than ever, for my pack to be happy, and I know her being beside me would help that. I can't say, now, what I want, because it's like a whole new world, like a whole new.... me has opened up." Axel almost had to hide his face in his hands. He was admitting some of this to himself only now.

Ingar hummed. "Yes, that's some of it. There's more. The bond grows. You'll never lose those things, though, or that curiosity about her. Assuming she lives."

That last comment cut Axel to the bone. From what he remembered of his grandfather, he was hyper-rational. And correct. Keira may not live. If they didn't find this cure, his time with her would only be a memory.

As if reading his mind, Chance said, "This is a lovely chat, family reunion, whatever, but we were sent here for a cure. Do you have a cave? A treasure chest? A chalice? Anything that might be hiding what we need? I assume Agnes isn't as batty as she appears."

"Oh, Agnes?" Ingar let out a raucous laugh. "I see. No, Agnes is the best of them, but her methods are... sometimes unorthodox." Then he became more somber. "Chance," he said, "are you bonded? Have you found your mate?" Chance huffed a little.

"No," he said. "I haven't really looked. It seems a little old fashioned."

There was silence for a while. Chance was looking at the three shifters who had been standing guard, eating around the other fire. Ingar gave Axel a look, and so neither said anything.

"I'm not even sure my mother and father were mates," Chance added. He stared into the fire.

"It's possible," Ingar said after a while. "I can't say what Graeme does next. I don't know who he has you with. Now he's barely more than a boy. I believe it would be disruptive if you were to see. But you're an alpha, right? It seems unlikely you didn't come from a bonded union. And we only bond mates."

Chance turned to Ingar. "You know my father? You don't want him dead?"

Again, Ingar laughed. "There is almost no one I want dead. Even the two of you, intruders, trussed up on those trees. It's the role of an alpha to act as though he would claw you through in a heartbeat, but you both know that's a very, *very* last resort, no?"

Chance shifted uncomfortably. Axel realized he had never really thought about it. His father had died suddenly, in an accident. There had been few lessons after the half-remembered ones from his grandfather.

"Have either of you ever killed anyone?" Ingar asked. "Shifter or human?"

"No," Axel said without hesitation. "Never." Chance shrugged.

"I don't think so," he responded. "Hurt badly, yes."

"So, you do know, then." Ingar sighed. He took another sip of the hard liquor, "You both must have had chances. Now let's just hope you haven't killed this poor girl."

This was worse than the paw to the head had been for Axel. He imagined, not for the first time, the breath leaving Keira's body. He imagined how he'd blame himself forever. He shook his head to himself. He couldn't imagine that life, the man he would become.

"Please," he said, "can you take us to Fairbanks? To the village, whatever there is now. Can you look with us for the cure?" Ingar smiled.

"No," he said. "My son is there. He's probably out drinking and being foolish as we speak. I don't think you should see him, Axel, not as he is now. And he shouldn't see you. And I don't want to see you react to anything else you might see." He turned to Chance. "Juneau, tell me more about this sister of yours. Tell me why you don't trust her to know her own mate." At the shocked look on Chance's face, Ingar screamed to his men,

Alpha's Enemy   97

"More food and drink, boys!" There was some grumbling from the other fire, but dark rye bread and another bag of jerky were brought over.

Chance took some of it all. He had thrown up everything inside him earlier, Axel recalled. And he had to agree, the alcohol was making this whole strange situation easier. When he was done chewing and had thrown back the liquid, Chance cleared his throat.

"I suppose she was always Dad's favorite." He stopped for a while. "Why do you need to know this?" Ingar rubbed his beard.

"How will I know what the cure might be if I don't know who is to be cured?" Axel and Chance both looked at him. "We're close to the Ambrosia Coven," he said. "Agnes may well assume I'll remember something that I don't in fact recall. But I could..." Another pause. "So, Chance, go on."

Chance closed his eyes for a moment.

"She was younger," he began, "so she was special. She was born very small. Always very blonde, always beautiful, even as a tiny undersized thing. I... I was big for my age. I sometimes resented the attention she got. I always loved her. Sometimes I got angry. She was my sister, *is* my sister, and when she was babied... I thought it would spoil her." He sighed, proffered up his glass to be filled, and drank. "Or maybe I was jealous, I don't know. She's cleverer than I am. As it turns out, I guess she might be tougher, too. Or at least, she might know her mind more."

Chance was drunk, just beginning to slur his words. Certainly, he was being the most honest Axel had ever heard. Axel didn't know whether he wanted to punch Chance or hug him. He didn't seem like the same guy who'd been squaring up to him earlier. Ingar saw it too, catching Axel's eye.

"So," he said, "you both want what's best for her? You both want her happy?"

"I never said any different!" Chance exclaimed.

22

CHANCE

Chance noticed, even in the dancing firelight, even after the drinks, that Ingar and Axel had the same eyes. Axel had a softer face: Ingar's cheekbones, but the heart-shaped face of his mother, whom Chance had glanced at only a few times when he was young. Ingar's questions raised Chance's hackles just a little, but the warmth and the drunkenness and the fear for his sister meant he spat out honesty.

"I'm afraid," Chance said. "I want what's best for her, but first, I want her to live. Okay?" Axel nodded.

"If I can never see her again," he said, "I still want her to live. I don't know how I'd do it... be without her... but I want her to be in the world." Ingar looked into the fire for a long while.

"Chance," he said. "Axel. Your packs have a feud? When was the last time they communicated? Met for a solstice or a general council meeting?"

Chance scoffed. He couldn't help himself. "Generations ago, surely?"

"No, boys." Ingar shook his head. "We do it now. We're in regular contact."

Alpha's Enemy   99

Chance didn't want to believe this. He ran his hand through his hair.

"That's not what my father told me!"

Axel muttered, "I don't remember..."

Ingar looked at the two young alphas. "You don't remember meeting as small children? Keira, too?"

Chance was uneasy. He had a vague idea of it having happened. He remembered the shape of Axel's mother's face...

"Sort of," Axel said. "I think Keira remembers."

"I'm guessing, of course," Ingar said, "but given your dates... Axel, if you know me, you'll know I never hated Juneau. Chance, your grandfather and I are good friends." Chance was drunk enough to lean forward at this.

"What?" A simple ripple of annoyance, not much more. "What about my father?" he asked. "He always told us to stay away from anything Fairbanks, that they'd double-crossed us a long time ago. I—" Axel turned to Chance. "I never asked!" he cried. "Did *you* ask for the details? I never did."

Ingar settled back, and he began to tell them a story—a story so much newer than either Axel or Chance had expected, and also so much simpler.

"There was this girl," Ingar started. "I know, it's the classic beginning to a story. There was this girl. A witch, in fact. A good friend of the Ambrosia Coven, though just visiting. This was a couple of years ago, and my son," he said, looking at Axel, "your father, Olliver, met the girl by chance. I had business with Ambrosia, and I took him with me. He is, as you of course know, to be the alpha when I die."

Ingar looked into the fire and rubbed his palms together. He was thinking about the vague new knowledge of his own demise that Chance and Axel represented, no doubt. And his son's. Chance shivered with the thought of his death, the thought of his sister's death, the idea of ever having a foreshadowing of his own. The alcohol was numbing him, and the fire was warm, yet this still got through.

Ingar cleared his throat. "Olliver met her while I had my business with the coven elders. A protection agreement between our pack, as we're closer to the sea, and their coven. Olliver was supposed to be sitting in, observing some easy diplomacy between allies, but the boy slipped off. He's a century old, almost, you'd think he would have his wits about him by now, but no, he saw a pretty girl down a corridor and off he went."

Knowing he was breaking into the story, vaguely, and that some respect should be shown for Axel's ancestor, Chance nonetheless let out, "So, what does this have to do with my father?"

Ingar raised his thick eyebrows. "I see alphas are almost cubs in the future. I hate to

think what things must have come to." He shot Axel a look that Chance couldn't read. Mocking Chance, or telling Axel this included him? The fire made it impossible to tell.

Then Ingar turned to Chance. "Your father—young Graeme. He fell for this little witch, too. I suppose she was a pretty thing. And neither of them are, well, experienced. Of course, they have been introduced to potential mates, but in the proper manner. This young witch was from a small island with its own ideas of what is proper.

Chance was busy wondering what 'proper' meant. How much had things changed for the shifters as the world had come up to meet them? And how much had his big gruff father changed in his short lifetime?

23

OLLIVER

Maybe it was the way she walked; the confidence in her strong legs; her strange, buckled shoes, the way her braid was wrapped around her head. Maybe it was being in the house of the Ambrosia Coven, one of the only permanent structures for miles around, and palpably thick with enchantments. Whatever it was, Olliver had to follow her.

His father was still making introductory niceties with the older witches. None of them were looking his way. The lanky young man, just beginning the slow, slow filling out that would leave him with his father's strong and slim build, stepped behind a staircase. As quietly as he could, he began down the corridor. His cloth and hide boots made almost no sound. But it was a long corridor, and he hadn't seen what door she'd gone into. She'd been halfway down when he turned to check on the attentions of his father, and once he'd slipped behind the staircase and into the corridor, she had been gone behind one of four doors.

The first, which was on his left, opened easily. The room was dim, a few of those witch-light lanterns glowing on the walls. It was full of piles of books and dust. The floor was a patchwork of rugs, and there were towering shelves, a double height ceiling or... Olliver looked up. Was there a ceiling at all? Uneasy with this idea, with books above him forever, Olliver stepped out of the room and closed the door a little too hard. He waited by it, not breathing.

On the other side of the corridor, the door opened to reveal a closet. It was chock-full of brooms, colorful cloaks, clogs, strange glass jars full of liquids, and an old crib. Olliver closed that door more quickly.

The third door was locked. He wriggled the handle gently. He put his ear to the wood. Nothing. Olliver let go of the handle. He took a step back and was about to move on when the door opened. It was her.

She was pale and had high, almond shaped eyes. Blue like his own. Her face was round, with some unruly strands of hair hanging down around it. Her clothing was strange: a thin draped fabric. When she spoke, her accent wasn't one he had ever heard before. It wasn't like the other witches' lilts or his father's rough, hard consonants.

"I heard two doors," she said. "This is the third?" Olliver could hardly speak. He nodded. She smiled, and her whole face lit up. "Well, three is a very magical number. Not as magical as seven, but it would be too much if you tried seven doors to find me." She opened the door wider. "Come in."

It was a bedroom. Olliver hesitated. He had never been into a girl's—a woman's— room before, other than his mother's and his sister's. He stepped in.

"Why were you listening for a door? Did you see me in the entryway?" he asked, hopeful that she had noticed him as he had her. She laughed a small, sweet laugh.

"I saw you for a moment, yes," she said. "And then I felt your

Alpha's Enemy 103

eyes on me. You know, a woman doesn't have to be a witch to feel that." She put out a hand. "Irna."

Olliver took her hand, and his stomach filled with a swirling murmur of birds.

"Hello, Irna," he said, "Olliver."

"You roll the 'r'," Irna noticed, "but no matter." She plopped down onto the wooden framed bed. "This mat is horsehair and straw," she said, wriggling a little. "It is very strange. At home, we use feathers. I don't know what they are called. The soft feathers from the chest of mother birds." She patted the bed next to her. "Sit!" she told him. "It isn't that bad."

Olliver's palms were sweating. "On, your bed?"

"Do you see anywhere else to sit?" Irna asked. "You are here with your father? To learn how to—" She fluttered her hands vaguely. "—do whatever it is the older ones do?" Olliver smiled. He found her so charming, so open.

"Yes," he said, sitting at the furthest end of the bed from Irna. "Diplomacy. It's a meeting. I come to a lot of them." Irna laughed that transformative laugh again.

"And they are boring?" Olliver nodded. "I am here to learn, too," Irna said. "I have come from my island, east, over the sea." She gestured vaguely in a direction that could easily, for all Olliver knew, have been east. "I am learning powerful enchantments to take back to my people." To Olliver's surprise, she rolled her eyes. "I do not know why they sent me. Maybe because of my age; it should be a long time until I die." Olliver was shocked at this, but Irna simply laughed again. "Olliver, you are so serious!" she said. "Today, we will not learn. We will sit here and talk, yes?"

Olliver's throat was dry. He nodded. "Yes, I would like to," he managed.

24

GRAEME

"Is there any more rye bread?" Graeme asked his mother, who was cooking over a fire just outside. She turned, sighed, and wiped her hands on her apron.

"Boy, you have your own home. Why not your own bread? Eating all of ours. Your siblings will go hungry." Graeme leaned against the low doorframe. He shrugged.

"You have to find me a wife, then I'll have bread." His mother let out a *tssk*.

"You have hands, no? Learn to bake or barter. Finding a mate isn't a matter of *deciding* to, from me or from you. It happens when it's supposed to. And you know that very well." Inside, his mother lifted a bag from the top of a shelf, untied it, and pulled out a loaf of dark bread. "Don't eat it all, Graeme, your father will be home soon. He has some business with Ambrosia this afternoon, and you know he needs to be well fed to deal with the coven!"

"They're spirited," Graeme laughed. Then he began to cut a slice of bread, pulling the butter across the table. He had only taken his first bite when his father came into the room. Lindan picked up the rest of the loaf and pocketed it.

"No time for lunch, son," he said, a hand coming down on Graeme's shoulder. "The Ambrosias have a visitor, and they are showing her around the systems they have helped us shifters with—a tour of the allied packs. And you are helping me lead ours."

Graeme groaned and shoved the slice of bread in his mouth.

"The Ambrosias treat me like a child," he complained. "I always feel like they are mocking me somehow."

"That's because they are," Lindan said. "Don't talk with your mouth full, for crying out loud. You're a grown man."

THE GROUP WAS WAITING in the main square: a couple of older witches Graeme vaguely recognized and a young woman he didn't, strangely dressed. She was wearing a kind of fur he'd never seen before and hard-soled boots with metal clasps. Her lips were pale pink, and her eyes were blue. She smiled at him and his father as they approached, though Graeme rather thought it was more at him.

"This," one of the older witches said as they came closer, "is Irna." She gestured to the younger woman. "She is visiting from the islands in the east to share some of our knowledge with her people. She's a powerful witch, but—" The elder Ambrosia witch looked at Lindan and raised her gray eyebrows. "—something of a handful."

Lindan nodded at her and pushed his son forward.

"Graeme will be showing you around," he said. "Hopefully he knows his way around the enchantments of his own village, but it's hard to tell with the young ones sometimes." The Ambrosia elder laughed. Graeme's ears burned. He took another step forward, this one very intentional.

"Shall we start with the bell tower?" he asked, pointing to the tallest of the wooden structures around the main square. "It allows us to communicate with other packs. The Ambrosia— Ah, your coven," he said, turning to the elders, "kindly built it for us to sound the alert for intruders of any kind, and also to call any rogue packs to battle. It's enchanted so it can be heard by all shifters."

Graeme was quite pleased with this explanation, but his father added, "Not, of course, that battles like that happen often. We try to stay friends with our neighbors."

Irna nodded. "Of course, as do we. But sometimes it can't be helped, hmm? My islanders are a very passionate people."

GRAEME WALKED the group of witches through the warm air that blew constantly around the village in the wintertime. He showed them the witch-lights that hung at various spots during the dark of falls and winters, the architectural tricks the coven had taught them, though these were not strictly magical. These, Irna waved away with a hand.

"My people have better ways for this," she said. "We have great halls with no enchantments whatsoever. We use earth and whole slim trunks and sometimes whalebones." She turned to Graeme. "Perhaps you should visit us some time? I am sure my people would love to have you!" She looked at Lindan. "It would season him, no? A trip?"

Lindan's noise was noncommittal, something between a grunt and a hum.

"That sounds— It sounds educational," Graeme said, wanting nothing more than to touch Irna's beautiful white skin and undo her strange braid.

"Enough of this," Lindan snapped. "You are all welcome to dine with us. Our great hall may not be much on yours, Irna, but it will fit your coven and my pack, and we have plenty ready to eat."

Graeme's heart was beating in his throat. He had been invited to her island. What did that mean? Was it to meet her people? Her parents? He thought about this for so long, he had to dash after all the others. Irna looked back as she heard his breath and his soft padding boots. She laughed.

"Head in the clouds, Graeme?" she asked. "I also have that problem sometimes."

Graeme thought he would do almost anything just to hear her say his name again.

25

IRNA

I t wasn't that she hadn't enjoyed her time in this snowy world, or the shifting people. They were interesting, as well as the relationship between the witches and their neighbors. But she would be glad to get back to her greener world and tell her people all the strange things she had seen.

Irna had learned that they were working on time-traveling. She hoped to one day come back to find out more about this. She doubted it was possible. She had many bundled parchments in her luggage, which was now being packed onto her small ship, where she would mostly sleep for the enchanted voyage home. She'd wake up to eat and drink water. The witchlight would change many things for the island, and enchantments for good harvests and quick forest growth were much needed.

When her family had sent her off, they had been worried she would be asked to stay. Irna didn't think the coven liked her at all, though. They thought she was strange, she was sure. And she was younger than any of them. She liked to wander off, it was true, but she wasn't work-shy. They just did things differ-

Alpha's Enemy

ently at home. There was less ceremony, so things took less time. And it seemed as though almost no one had liked her jokes. No, Irna would be glad to get home.

She turned to see how the packing of her boat was going. She wanted to help, but the coven had insisted on hiring some local men to do it. She suspected they hadn't even lightened the packages for them.

Imelda was busy casting enchantments on the boat. Irna walked over to her.

"Thank you," she said. Imelda seemed annoyed. She finished her spell, muttering, a birch branch with a split end in her hand. That was something Irna thought was silly. They didn't need those branches. It was, she knew, for show.

"Hmm?" Imelda turned to her.

"Thank you," Irna repeated, "for housing me and for teaching me." She opened her arms and walked forwards, going to hug Imelda. No arms came back for her. Imelda was stiff as a board, arms and birch branch by her sides. Irna stepped back, embarrassed, happier than ever to be going home.

"Well," Imelda said. "It's been a— We're glad to have helped. A long way back, all us witches come from the same place. A long way back." Then she turned, still stiff, and nodded to the boat. "All should be ready. Goodbye, Irna. We'll wave you off, of course."

Waves, but not hugs. Obviously.

Irna was just beginning to walk toward her boat when she felt a hand on her shoulder, panting in her ear.

"Irna—" Olliver was out of breath. Irna turned.

"You rolled my 'r'!" she exclaimed. Olliver was pink-faced from exertion.

"Of course." He put his hands on his hips. "Wow, I was sure I would miss you. I wanted to say... well... goodbye, and..."

Irna grinned, and Olliver's eyelids fluttered. His eyes were so wide and blue. She thought he would grow into a fine man, when he started laying down some muscle and fat onto his bones. Then she pulled him into a bear hug.

"Goodbye, Olliver. Thank you! Thank you!" Irna let out a squeal and let Olliver go. Graeme was here, too! He was standing a little way away, a bag in his hand. He put up a hand in a wave, but Irna ran to him. "Graeme! You also came to say goodbye?" She hugged him just as tight as she had Olliver. This was like a last-minute reprieve. The young people were not as strange as the old! Her friends had come to say goodbye. They had spoken to her openly, almost been funny.

"Yes," Graeme said, hugging back. "Yes, but also... well, I could come... to visit your home?" They broke away from the hug, and Irna nodded fervently. She held Graeme still, away from her now. He was like one of the farm boys from home. He would never be as imposing as his father, but his face was kind and his golden hair was like the hair of most of her people. Perhaps this was why he made her feel safe.

"Yes! Of course!" She dragged him a little closer to Olliver. "We will arrange it when I am home. You both must come!" She squeezed their arms. "But now, I must go!" Irna hugged them both at once, one boy in each arm. "Wave me off, yes?" Then she ran into the surf, to her vessel.

～

As Irna's boat began to gain speed, Irna used her last waking moments to look up above the prow. She wanted to wave to her friends.

But the boys weren't there. Two bears seemed to be fighting on the shore. The red of blood from scratches and bites was running out into the water, coloring the foam.

Alpha's Enemy 111

Irna was going to call, to sit up properly and take a better look, but the enchantment overcame her, and she dropped down into blankets and furs and slept.

26

AXEL

Axel leaned toward Ingar. "You're telling us this whole rivalry—this whole... the reason for years of hate and for Keira's life hanging in the balance—is because our fathers were into the same girl?"

"Into?" Ingar raised his eyebrows questioningly. "If you mean they shared an infatuation, then yes. They did."

Chance scoffed. "I don't believe you. That's not enough! My father was more sensible than that!"

"Was he?" Ingar asked, "He isn't now, I can tell you that. And neither is my son. They got into a fight over her. More than a scuffle. They were lucky the witches were around to heal them, or else either or both could be dead." Axel bit his lower lip. At least his own mess was about his mate.

"But she couldn't have been bonded to either of them. She wasn't... isn't a shifter. Why would they fight over her?"

Ingar laughed. "Hurt pride? I can't tell you. I don't know. High blood and youth. Embarrassment, maybe. She didn't want either of them, and they both felt the need to prove their power and their masculinity. Only they can answer. If you asked them now, they wouldn't tell you, and in your time, I'm afraid you are too late.

Axel's head was spinning. The time travel, the alcohol, the smoke from the fire, the idea of his father as a foolish young man making mistakes... But worse, his father standing by those mistakes later, letting them harm Axel, Chance, Keira, two whole packs.

"I know," Ingar told Chance and Axel, "your fathers are not people to you. Not really. At least not people who could have made such grave mistakes. But we all change, and we can all be stupid. Hell, my first instinct was to claw you two in half. I told you that. We learn to control ourselves, to make better decisions. Perhaps your fathers died before they had finished that growing." It was hard to see in the dimming firelight, but Axel was almost sure Ingar wiped his eyes.

"Why should we believe you?" Chance questioned. "How do we know any of this is real? We might be asleep on the floor of the Ambrosia House, or you might be lying to us about this entire situation." Ingar smiled, apparently recovered from his moment of emotion.

"I thought you might ask that." He put a hand in either pocket and drew out two pieces of parchment.

Axel and Chance moved closer to see them. In Ingar's left hand was the scroll they had brought, unmistakable, its Ambrosia seal carefully broken, the parchment brown with age and the ink of its message fading to yellowish. In his right was a flat piece of parchment without seal. It was brand new, roughly pressed, still stiff. The marks of ink on it were clear. Both parchments bore the same message.

THE PACKS of the Southeastern Territories of the Northern Lands will forever remain united in friendship.

No dispute, no marriage, no quarrel or war will break this alliance. This is, has, and always will be true.

Signed, Northern alphas: Lindan of the east, Ingar of the south.

On this day, October 15, 1618.

"This one," Ingar said, holding up the new parchment, "was signed just last week by myself and Lindan. This," he said, holding up the old one, "was, as you will have deduced, given to you by your own Ambrosia Coven. I don't know what happened to it in the meantime, but I have kept it with me since it was written up, and I intend for it to be stashed with my will and testament. I would rethink where I secrete it, but I know that what has been and what is and what will be... are. And you are here now."

Axel could hardly breathe. What did this mean for him and Keira? It depended on Chance, he supposed, and on finding that cure.

"Perhaps it has been leading up to this," Ingar went on. "There will be a bonding ceremony when you return to your time. Our clans will be one."

Chance let out something oddly like a squeak. Then he said, "We need to find that cure, or there's no chance of any of that."

Axel nodded his head, although had no idea if anyone saw. Ingar smiled, like he knew some great secret. Perhaps he did.

"Yes," he said, "my alpha-cubs. The fire is dying down, and the food and drink are gone. Let's head to the Ambrosia Coven and see what they can do." He stood and stretched, looking almost like another dark-shadowed tree. "We're too tired and too intoxicated to shift. We will take the sleds."

Ingar called to his men, who kicked snow over their own fire and then over the fire the three alphas had been sitting around. The six men headed down a dark path, barely

Alpha's Enemy 115

discernable through the trees. For a moment, it occurred to Axel to be worried, but he batted this away. He knew that Ingar believed them. What else had the last few hours been about? They had been tied to trees, helpless. Ingar wouldn't let them down to toy with them. He wondered if Chance knew this.

When they were in step, he muttered to his companion, "You okay?"

"Think so," came Chance's calm reply. Axel was surprised at how measured he sounded. After only five or so minutes of walking, they heard the rough barks of the dogs. The beautiful white and grey creatures soon came into view, huddled for warmth, wagging their tales to see their masters.

Axel knew dog sleds well. They both still had huskie packs and had regularly used them for medium-distance transport before ATVs and snowmobiles. But not since their very youngest days had they been on wooden sleds with hide covered seat-backs, rushing through forest pathways. It was amazing what the body unlearned, Axel thought as he worried about his expensive jacket ripping on the branches. He tried to remember how to lean against the turns with no seatbelt and no give of fiberglass and modern alloy.

Both Axel and Chance were swearing under their breaths.

"Is that normal language, when you're from?" asked Ingar with the slightest bit of haughtiness.

"Actually, it pretty much is," Chance replied against the wind, and Axel had to shout his agreement.

"You know how fast things change now, Grandfather?" Ingar grunted in the affirmative. "They change a thousand times faster when we're from." Axel paused, unsure whether he should finish. In the end, he added, "Don't worry, you'll see some of it."

"Not the iPhone, though!" Chance yelled. "Lucky for him."

Axel laughed.

"Right. You know Byron was proud of sending that emergency text, because his is pretty much for show."

Chance cackled.

"I was wondering what that was all about! We have some that are the same!"

"Well," Ingar said, "looks like there are some things I will never understand, and this conversation is one of them."

27

CHANCE

The dogs knew to wait at the gates of the Ambrosia House. It took a few minutes, but when the witch got there, she greeted Ingar and opened the gates. The two shook hands.

"Imelda," said Ingar.

"Ingar," said the witch, Imelda.

There were balls of orange light dancing up the driveway, illuminating them all dimly. Not competing well with the night. Ingar and the witch walked up front, heads close together. No doubt he was explaining what they had come for.

"Why do I feel like a child in trouble with his teacher?" Axel asked Chance, who chuckled.

"I think that's what this is, right? Our elders disapprove."

Axel sighed. "Seems like it's our elders who made the mess."

Chance said nothing, but silently, he agreed. If this was true, it made a mockery of his entire time as alpha, of his beliefs about his father, himself, his pack... and about Keira and Axel.

They stepped into the entryway of the Ambrosia Coven's house. It was the same house they had been in earlier—or, Chance thought, later—but nothing was as big. There were fewer branching corridors. The lights were all those floating orbs, which gave everything a warm glow but also made it hard to see details. It was still a large and confusing and potentially illusionary space. Just on a slightly smaller scale.

Perhaps it was because the light was dim, but the witch who had collected them from the gate came very close up to their faces. She looked at Axel, her eyes very wide, her eyebrows and wild hair just like Agnes', though she was older.

"Oh, yes," she said to Ingar. "He's yours, isn't he? Strong family resemblance." She raised her bushy eyebrows at Ingar. "Good for you. He's a looker. Is he as intelligent?" Ingar smiled serenely.

"It would be rude to say in front of them, Imelda." The witch seemed to gather herself and remember she wasn't just with an old friend.

"Of course." She stood up straighter, turning to Chance. "And you," she said, "a Harstrom! My goodness, you have that same resolve in your eyes. Green is never to be fully trusted. In nature, it comes and goes with the seasons. I hope you make it work for you, young alpha." The old witch stood and looked them up and down a while longer, and then she said, "Come," ushering them down the corridor in front of them.

To Chance's surprise, after a few minutes' walk, they ended up in what seemed to be the same living room they had left from. There was a fire burning in the grate. The room was large and grand, as before, except that the furniture was far more rustic, and the sconce lights had been replaced by those balls of hanging orange. Chance looked at Axel, questioning. Axel shrugged.

"Do you have a cure?" Chance demanded. "Did Ingar explain?"

Imelda smiled. Her lips were chapped. "Of course he

Alpha's Enemy

explained. There has been strife between you two, no? Your packs?"

"Yes," Alex said, both he and Chance nodding. "But that's not —" Imelda waved a hand at him.

"Oh, it is!" she chirped. "You know, I was there, just a few years ago, when your fathers had that ridiculous fight. The girl, she was gifted; she was beautiful. I can see why they fell for her. But she was flighty, and she was going home. She was homesick the entire time she was here. We would hear her crying sometimes at night. And those boys... She wanted their friendship, probably still does. They nearly ripped one another to pieces and got their wounds full of dirty seawater and grit. It was lucky we were there."

"Right," Chance said, "Ingar told us. But if you can fix them, why can't you fix Keira?"

"Oh!" Imelda laughed again. "We can. Of course."

"You can now, but can't you in the future? In our time?" Ingar handed Chance the scroll they had arrived with, tied back up, this time in a bow.

"Of course!" Imelda said. "Apparently, we only get wilier. I'm proud of the sister who sent you to us."

Ingar nodded his assent. Imelda pulled a birch branch from her robes, its end a fork. She began to whisper incantations.

"No!" Chance cried. "What are you doing?"

Just as he was about to ask if it was a spell of protection or something to take back to Keira, Ingar called, "Goodbye, you two! Good luck!"

Chance felt what seemed to be hands on his shoulders. He looked at Ingar, at Axel, as if they might have been the hands of one of the men, and the last thing he saw before his feet were ripped from beneath him was the whites of Axel's eyes.

～

LANDING on a wooden floor was different from landing in a snowdrift.

"Ah!" Chance shouted when his back thumped into the floor.

Seconds later, Axel landed on the sofa, yelled, and rolled off onto a rug.

"Jesus!" Chance exclaimed. "What if we'd landed in the fire?" Agnes, who was cross-legged on an armchair, shrugged.

"Very unlikely," she said, "given the size of this room. And of this house." She thought for a second. "Inside a wall would be *more* likely. And then I suppose you'd suffocate." The witch smiled, and Chance hadn't the slightest idea whether or not she was joking.

"What the hell, Agnes?" Axel almost yelled as he jumped up to his feet. "We were looking for— Why didn't you tell us what we were looking for? Why do I feel like I've been taken for a fool?"

Chance was pleased to see some anger from Axel. It had been lacking from his fellow alpha, like Chance had been cursed with carrying it all.

"We don't have anything," Chance said. "All that happened was talking, and then, a witch— Imelda, she—"

"Ah!" Agnes smiled. "Aunt Imelda. Always a little severe, eh?"

"We don't have the cure!" Chance screamed. He was sure his sister must be near death already. He could hardly breathe thinking of it; imagining her face, her slowed breathing...

"Is she?" Axel chipped in. "Is she still alive? Can we see her? I need to see her!" Chance felt no annoyance at Axel's demands. Not this time. He seconded the need.

"Right," he said, "let me see my sister. Let us see Keira."

"So you're a 'we' now? A team?" Agnes asked, still sitting casually on her chair. Chance rubbed his hand through his greasy hair. When had they last slept, apart from being knocked

Alpha's Enemy

unconscious by strange shifters in the past? He could barely think.

"For this," Axel replied, "yes. You made us a team. But obviously, you were wrong, because we failed. We have nothing." He opened his palms to show they were empty. Chance pulled the scroll out of his pocket and threw it at Agnes' feet.

"Here's this back. Fat lot of good it did." Then he and Axel flopped down on the sofa, bone tired. They began to pull off their outdoor clothes, sweltering in the heat of the fire, piling them on the sofa beside them.

28

AXEL

Picking up the rolled parchment and sitting down on the armchair with her feet to the floor, like a normal person, Agnes grinned. "I see Ingar got this?"

"How...?" Axel was too tired to even finish his sentence. All he wanted was to see Keira. He could feel her near, like she was calling to him. Her body was calling to his. Even if these were his last moments with her, he needed them. He would pack them up and keep them with him as long as he lived.

Agnes pointed at the bow on the parchment. "I only knew Ingar in his later years, but he was always very neat. Good with knots. I would tease him for it."

"I'm going to see her, Agnes." Axel stood up. "I don't have time for this." Chance was right behind him, standing as well. Axel put a hand on his shoulder, a thanks for the solidarity or something. They hadn't taken a step when Agnes got to her feet.

"You will see her when I say you can see her," the witch boomed. She seemed much taller than before. Axel didn't know whether it was shock or magic that made both Chance and himself quickly sit down again. "You will see Keira again. Soon," Agnes said. "First, tell me what Ingar told you." There was a pause as the men waited on one another to speak. Then Chance spoke, once again in his gruff and grumpy voice.

"Well, first his men knocked us out and tied us to trees."

"You could have warned us," Axel added. "About a few things, actually."

Agnes Ambrosia, back to being petite and sitting cross-legged, her hair large and wild, smiled and shrugged. "It would have defeated the point, which I'm surprised you haven't grasped yet."

Axel looked at Chance, Chance at Axel. They were both too worn down and worried to have their heads messed with.

"What?" Axel demanded. "What's the point?" Agnes allowed for a dramatic pause. Witches were so irritating.

"What did you learn from Ingar?"

"Our fathers were fighting over a girl," Chance answered. "They were young and stupid. Our lives have been a damn lie." Agnes nodded slowly.

"A little harshly put, but essentially, yes."

"Hang on," Axel said, the fog clearing from his brain for a moment. "The parchment. The new parchment. That parchment, but before. What happened to it? Its binding, where did it go?" Agnes waved the aged version of the agreement between Axel's and Chance's tribes.

"Its binding?" she echoed. Axel looked at Chance.

"Where was it?" Chance asked. Agnes put the parchment down, seemingly shelving her question for later.

"Buried," she said. "Axel, your father buried it. It was in a box, safe from decay. Perhaps he knew one day he would want it, get over his childish feud. But he didn't live to see that day." She glanced at Chance. "Don't get any ideas, Harstrom. Your father would have done just the same. Anyway, the box was dug up where they're building new storage space a little out of town."

"Why was it not brought to me?" Axel questioned. The witch stood up and handed over the piece of parchment.

"What would you have done two weeks ago, if this had been given to you?"

"I..." Axel swallowed. "I would have... I would have called a meeting."

"And then?" the small witch prompted. Axel stared at Chance, whose gaze was on the floor. "Your friend Byron is a sensible man, Axel," Agnes continued. "And he knows the ways of these woods well. You're right to keep him close. He'd make a valuable advisor. His eldest son was at work on the site. When Byron saw the parchment, he brought it to us for verification. Then this whole business with Keira..."

Axel's mind leapt back to his mate, and he felt awful, gut-wrenched to have been thinking of anything else. Agnes saw the look on Axel's face, which was probably mirrored on Chance's.

"Keira," she said, "was the missing piece of the puzzle. Her and the parchment, together, were the key. What has been—"

"Yes," Axel interrupted, becoming increasingly irritated with the witch. "Time is fixed but nonlinear. We get it." Beside him, Chance smiled.

Agnes looked as though she might do the big and booming thing again, and Axel tensed up. But she merely returned to her speech, in a slightly more irritated tone.

"Yes. And neither the parchment nor Keira and Axel's bond would have worked alone. You needed both." Again, the witched paused. She walked back to her chair but didn't sit down. She just picked up a cardigan that was hung there. "I will let you see Keira, on one condition."

"Yes," Chance said at the same time Axel said, "Fine."

"Tell me how you feel about one another?"

Chance and Axel looked at each other, wondering who would start. Finally, Axel was the one to begin.

"Chance cares deeply for his sister and his pack. He can be funny, but not always at the right times, and he may have slight anger issues. He leads in a different way to me, but he's a good leader. I... I respect him, I suppose." Axel was about to avoid Chance's eyes, then realized how childish that would be. Instead, he nodded at the man who had been his teammate through so much.

Chance cleared his throat. "Sometimes, Axel can be... well... a wuss. Often, he's right about thinking things through, though. He would do anything for his pack. His family seems to be strong and loving... and he is my sister's mate, there's no question of that."

Agnes clapped her hands together.

"Finally!" Then she pointed at the parchment now resting on the sofa's armrest. "And that contract is binding?" Again, the men exchanged a glance. Agnes took this as a yes, apparently. "Keira is fine," she said. "She's been healing since the moment she arrived. Do you see? Keira and Axel's bond, the parchment... This all had to happen, was destined to happen, to unite your packs as they have always previously been united. You were one when you came to Alaska—all you shifters were. Petty jealousies stand in your way. You can be far too close to human sometimes."

Both men had stood up and were barely listening to the witch. They were incoherently shouting at the same time.

"How dare you trick us!"

"Take us to her now!"

Agnes put a finger to her lips to shush them, and Axel and Chance were quiet. "It worked, didn't it?"

29

KEIRA

Keira opened her eyes. She had been in and out of consciousness since she had arrived at Ambrosia House. She had been surrounded by various witches —young and old, casting incantations and removing bandages —and Byron, always sitting in the chair by her bedside, sleeping or reading, ready to say, "Hi, sleepyhead," or "Any better?"

This time, the curtains had been opened. It was one of the few sunny hours of the day, and white fall light tumbled into the room. It didn't even hurt Keira's eyes. She put her hands under the covers, which were clean and fresh and must have been changed during her latest bout of unconsciousness. Nothing. No bandages, no pain. She was still drowsy, but that was about it.

Keira smiled and turned on her side to greet Byron. Instead, she found Chance in the armchair, looking beyond exhausted. His hair was greasy, and he had bags so dark, they were almost bruises under his eyes. He was smiling.

"I hate to say it, sis, but in that weird nightgown, and in this light, you look a bit like an angel." Keira laughed, glad to find she could without pain.

Alpha's Enemy   127

"Chance." She said his name quietly, her voice feeling very unused. "You look awful. What happened?"

Chance leaned forward. "You did."

"Ugh, you smell as bad as you look." Chance wiped his eyes with the heels of his hands.

"Yes, it's tears," he said. "You nearly died or whatever, and we had to go back in time. It was this whole thing." Keira laughed.

"You what?" Chance waved a hand. The explanations could come later. Suddenly, though, Keira's face went dark. "Oh, Chance, I'm sorry. This was my fault. I was shifted too long... I barely remember it. I ate a rabbit, and then I was looking for you and Axel, and when I saw you, I couldn't stop myself. I wanted to stop you fighting, but not like that."

Chance had a hand on his sister's elbow. "We can talk about it later, Keira, but please know it wasn't your fault. On this one, it's useless to apportion blame, but we can probably shift it to all three of us."

Keira cocked her head at the mentioning of the three of them. Chance nodded to the other side of the bed. Keira turned her head. Axel was asleep on his chair, leaning forward so that his head was on the edge of her bed, his fingers twitching with dreams, close to where hers had been lying in her sleep. Keira let out a small gasp. She turned back to Chance.

"You're in the same room? Both alive?" Chance smiled.

"I like him better when he's asleep, but I can deal with him awake. We got some new information while you were catnapping. And we were forced to spend some time together. I'll let him explain." He leaned over and pulled his sister into a hug. "That doesn't hurt, does it?"

"No," she said, pressing her face against his chest, "not at all." The last time they'd hugged, Keira thought, had been their father's funeral.

"I love you, Keira," Chance muttered, halfway to his favorite gruff tone, pulling away from the hug and laying his sister softly back down in her pillows.

"Love you, bro," Keira said, a cheeky smile on her lips. Chance stood up.

"I'm going to leave you two alone," he said. "I think Agnes said something about a privacy enchantment or something, but I'll check. I don't want to hear anything." Chance walked slowly across the room, clearly exhausted. At the door, one hand on the handle, he turned. "By the way, I give you my blessing. You and Axel can be bonded, whenever you like. As soon as we can sort out the details of the ceremony with Fairbanks, if you want. I think our clans are going to make a good team. And I think you're going to be very happy."

As Chance closed the door, Keira felt she must be either dreaming or dead. What had happened in the few days she'd been sleeping? When she turned herself to where Axel was asleep, she almost expected him to be gone. He was still there. He'd moved slightly since the last time she'd looked, so now his head was to the side, his hair falling across his face. Keira laced her fingers with his and felt that warm tingle of electricity, of light passing between them. With her other hand, she brushed back his dirty hair.

Axel's eyes flickered open. His lips were chapped. Keira traced them with her thumb. He smiled and kissed it. "I fell asleep, I'm sorry. I was waiting for you..."

"It's okay. You look so tired," Keira said, pulling his hand against her chest. "I just spoke to Chance." Axel made to sit up, to look over at the other chair, but Keira pulled him down. "It's okay," she said, "he wanted to give us some privacy." She kissed Axel's knuckles, one by one.

"I missed you," Axel said. "I really thought— I'm so sorry." Keira shook her head.

"Let's not do blame, okay? How long was I out?"

"Very hard for me to say." Axel laughed lightly and yawned. Keira followed suit.

"You're infectious," she said.

"You're tired."

Keira nodded and pulled on Chance's hand. "Get in with me? It's big enough."

"I would get in a single sleeping bag with you, Keira, I don't care how big the bed is." Keira let go of his hand.

"Take off your top," she said. "I want to see you. Feel your skin." Obediently, Axel stood, pulling off his long-sleeved shirt and undoing his belt, dropping it on the floor.

"Just so it doesn't scratch you," he said. Keira raised her eyebrows but said nothing. Axel slipped under the covers and put his arms around her, and she nuzzled into his neck. "I must smell awful," Axel said, "I haven't showered."

"No," Keira said, "you smell extra like Axel. I like it." She pushed her body toward his. "I like it a lot." She wasn't lying. The smell of her mate was intoxicating. She kissed his shoulder to taste his skin and ran her hands up and down his back to feel the muscle there, the few faint scars. To check he was real and all accounted for and hers. Every atom in her body seemed to be tingling, shining, doing new things.

"Does anything hurt, still?" Axel asked. "Are you okay?"

"I'm with you. I'm perfect. This is perfect." Keira pulled back to look at him. "I love you, Axel. More than I can possibly say." Axel smiled and kissed her.

"I love you, too. I went back in time for you, Keira. There were these... Well, my pack, and we got knocked out. Your brother is not so bad."

"Axel," Keira sighed. "Please don't talk about my brother in bed."

"Right." Axel grinned. "New rule, no talking about Chance in bed. I should have guessed that one." Gently, Keira twisted Axel's hair around her fingers and pulled.

"You should have," she muttered. "Are you both serious about time travel? Why?"

Now, Axel nuzzled her. She flipped over to be the little spoon, letting him push her hair away from her neck to nibble and lick. She was having a hard time not moaning. Axel paused to speak.

"I'll tell you the story better tomorrow, I'm sure, but the coven had to show us something because they knew it was the only way we would believe it. Your father and mine fought over a girl. *That's* the feud. And our grandfathers signed a pact to stay allies. It was hidden. By my father, actually."

This was an awful lot of information to take in with the heat of Axel pushing against her.

"Also," he went on, "you and I are part of... healing the rift?"

"Like, destiny?" Keira laughed. Axel hummed in agreement.

"Pretty much, actually. There's something about time and it being fixed but nonlinear. But destiny is easier to say." Axel's hand had found its way under her nightdress and was playing with her breast. "Is this okay?" he murmured in her ear.

"Keep your hand there forever," Keira told him, "as your other hand is here." She pulled his free hand down between her thighs. Axel moaned at the feel of her wetness. He pulled her closer into him, and she could feel him pressing against his pants, against her buttocks. "Axel," Keira breathed while she could still talk, "Chance gave us his blessing. If you want to—"

"Oh, god, yes." Axel pushed his fingers into her, kissing her jawline. "Of course."

Keira pulled Axel's hand from between her thighs and flipped over to face him. She yanked the nightdress off over her head and wriggled out of her underwear.

Alpha's Enemy

"Axel," she said, "do I have to take your pants off for you?"

"Are you okay? Are you well?" Keira smiled at his look of concern.

"Look at me," she told him. There was not a scratch on her body, save for some silvery scars running down her sides and across her flat stomach. Axel traced them with his fingers, still damp from her. As Axel wasn't doing it, Keira began to undo his pants. Axel helped, and he wriggled out of them and his boxer shorts. Keira stroked him, hard and warm and ready. She looked him in the eyes as she did it.

"I've barely been conscious," she said, "but every part of me has missed you."

Axel pulled her up to him, their mouths meeting, warm and wonderful. Keira wrapped a leg around him, pulling him close to her, loving the feeling of him pressing into her stomach, until he took her by the thighs and shifted her up. He slid inside her, making them both groan with pleasure.

Axel's hand came up to her butt, pushing, controlling the slow motion of their lovemaking. They were both so sleepy, it was almost like dreaming. Slower and sweeter and fuller of warmth and light than before. Again, Keira lightly pulled Axel's hair, watching as he bit his lip. They were on their sides, and she could feel him filling her, completing her somehow.

Keira thought she could stay like this forever: the sun on her back, Axel pushed against her, inside her, his hands on her and hers on him. In a way, she supposed she would. This thought excited her, and she began to move a little faster. Axel moaned, pulling her hair now. He said her name in her ear, full of love and want.

He ducked down again and put his mouth to her breast just as their strokes grew faster. That was it. It overcame her. The warmth below her belly extended, washed over her, became that electricity from before. She arched her back and pulled him into her, and he moaned, too, pushing his face into her neck, saying her name again and again.

30

AXEL

It didn't matter that it was happening in the dead dark of winter. In fact, that made the orbs of floating witch light (requested by Axel) all the more striking. There was a rare clear sky, and the stars were like a reflection of the ice that coated the town below.

Well, time was fixed and also nonlinear, and so maybe up was down sometimes. Axel certainly felt upside down and inside out. It wasn't as though he hadn't spent every moment since his return to the present with Keira, but today was going to change everything. They were going to be bonded, forever, and he had not a single doubt about it being right.

"Nervous?" Byron asked. "Your hair is getting all messed up. Bend down."

"You're such a dad sometimes," Axel said, but he bent to let his friend smooth back his unruly hair.

"I am a dad," said Byron. "Hey, and now it's your duty to produce an heir. Try and make your first kid a girl? I think we could do with a female alpha."

"Wow," Axel said, "burdening me with children before I've

even had a chance to enjoy my bonding, and now you're killing me, too." Byron shrugged.

"Just saying, less machismo over the last few centuries could have saved us all a lot of trouble." Axel had to agree with him.

"You aren't wrong. If I have a son, I'll just get parenting tips from you, though. You had things under control pretty much the whole time." They were reaching the town hall. Axel turned to Byron. "Thank you," he said, "for everything. I mean it."

Byron clapped his friend on the arm. "I know you do. And you'd better!"

"I'm showing you, aren't I?"

The two men walked up the steps to the hall and pushed open the door. At the end of a row of chairs, by a podium, stood a group of men and a few women, mostly looking to be in their thirties or forties, along with a couple past middle age. In the middle, leaning on the podium, was Chance, who waved to Axel and Byron, raised his eyebrows, and smiled.

"Right," Axel muttered to Byron, "let's get this over with so we can get to the real stuff." The elders let Axel through with no problem but huffed a little at standing aside for Byron. "Enough of that, he's about to be one of yours," Axel said.

"Hey!" Chance greeted him. "Nervous for later?"

"Not at all." Axel started looking over the paper.

"Right answer. So let's just sign this and get on with it, eh? I've leafed through it. Accord, blah, blah, peace and union, blah, blah, Byron initiated into the council and official Mediator of the packs, something about our heirs, male or female, blah, blah." Byron shot Chance a look. "I'm kidding! We all got sent a copy, of course I read it all. Just checking this one's the same. All three copies in all three safes better be watertight! I'm not having anyone burying it for a hundred years and having our kids at one another's throats."

"Might be too soon for that joke, Chance," Axel said, but he

Alpha's Enemy 135

was trying to suppress a smile. Byron leaned over Axel as he looked through the document.

"Looks good," he said. Chance turned to the council members surrounding the trio.

"We good to go?" he asked. Solemnly, they nodded.

A box was opened, and a wooden fountain pen was brought out from its velvet-lined insides. One by one, Chance, Axel, and, on an earlier page, Byron, signed the document. Axel put the pen back in the box.

"Hope the next bit of today feels more exciting than this." He turned to Chance. "Maybe we should hug?"

"Don't push it, we're not family yet. Is it okay if I apologize for trying to recruit your cheating ex to spite you in my speech later?"

This time, Byron laughed. "Chance, you're so much funnier now that you aren't trying to kill us."

As the three younger men walked away from the podium, the members of the council were muttering among themselves. Some of them had been covering for the actions of Chance's and Axel's fathers, and that was something they were going to deal with in coming weeks. But it wasn't a thought for now.

31

KEIRA

Keira wasn't waiting impatiently, or with any kind of worry. In fact, she'd helped herself to a beer from behind the bar, and now she was sitting on a bar stool, her dress tucked up under her, her snow boots showing. She hadn't seen Axel all day, though, and she missed him. She never thought she would feel that for anyone, that she would miss them because they weren't there when she woke up in the morning.

Keira had always been a bed hog, waking up splayed like a starfish, covers in a pile on the floor or all pulled over her, with any partner she'd had squished against the wall or freezing cold or both. With Axel, her body wanted to be close to his. It was as though their bodies remembered one another from the first moment they had touched.

She shook her head. She was about to have her bonding ceremony. She shouldn't be thinking about sex. Or should she? She had no idea, never having done this before. She looked at her phone and drained her beer, wondered if she should have another one. Would it be uncouth to smell like lager as Agnes tied the bonding rope around their wrists? Probably not, actually—it was Agnes Ambrosia, after all.

The guests had begun arriving a little while ago, shooting odd looks at her sitting there at the bar. And by 'guests,' Keira meant almost the entirety of the two packs. It was about to be standing room only at Byron's, though it seemed larger in the bar area than usual. Had Agnes done a little something extra when she and her coven were decorating?

There was no witch light in Byron's, but there were what looked like either fairy lights or stars twisting their way all over the place, even up the walls, like vines.

"Not too much," had been Keira and Axel's instructions, and they had been half listened to by the witches, who, egged on by Agnes, were sure this was all their doing. And she supposed they were mostly correct. Keira and Axel would be on the run without them, or worse, one or both of them would be—

Well, they weren't, so there was no need to think about it.

Assessing the number of people already in the bar, Keira hopped down and began to make her way toward the areas that usually held the dart boards. Now, it was all hung in cream and more of those lights. Keira wanted to lift the light fabric and see if the boards were still underneath, but she held herself back. In front of that was the traditional arch of twisted birch and yew, which the couple would step through once they were tied together, symbolizing moving into a new life with each other.

Once upon a time, back when the shifters had more rules about morality, they would have stepped through it into their marital home, where Axel would have taken her maidenhead. Or whatever. Even in that scenario, Keira couldn't imagine them getting further than the stairs.

"Psst," a voice whispered from behind the cream fabric behind her. Keira jumped. She lifted it. No dartboards. Instead, there was a small room that hadn't been there before, hiding

Agnes Ambrosia, wearing a cloak, with feathers in her hair. "Nervous?" she asked.

"No, just impatient," Keira replied.

"Excellent!" said Agnes. "Just had to check. Because if you were nervous, I'd have to get you out of here ASAP. Can't bind a couple who aren't true mates. Believe me, I've seen it done. Leads to all sorts of disasters. Especially if they're stubborn and have children."

This was not the rousing pep talk Keira had been expecting, but again, it was Agnes. The witch suddenly cocked her head to the side.

"Ooh," she said, "nearly time. Positions, I think!"

In a binding ceremony, the woman stands and waits for the man. The man has to ask, proffering his wrist.

Keira was in a green dress. She'd argued that it clashed with her eyes, but it was the way things were done. Green for a good harvest; fertility.

"Not yet," she'd said when she was being fitted and had this explained. The old Fairbanks woman tutted and said something about the young ones these days.

Then there was the 'ding' of the door opening. A customer— or, in this case, her brother, her watcher, and her mate.

The crowd was thick but quietened down, and it split to let Axel through. His suit was blue, watering the green crops, though he'd insisted on a darker shade than was usually used. Not that Keira cared what either of them was wearing. She couldn't help a grin spreading across her face as he walked toward her. Byron was smiling, too, and Chance gave her a thumbs up.

When Axel reached her, he touched her face and proffered his wrist, and she couldn't stop herself from grabbing his hand

Alpha's Enemy

and pulling him toward her. She needed his mouth on hers before they did this, as indecent as it was.

"You taste like beer," he murmured as they drew away from one another. And he smiled. Then he put out his wrist again, and Agnes stepped forward with the binding rope.

~

WHAT TO READ NEXT
Code of the Alpha: Shifter Romance Collection
One dark secret. Five sexy shifters.

OTHER BOOKS YOU WILL LOVE

Code of the Alpha: Shifter Romance Collection
One dark secret. Five sexy shifters.

Royal Dragon Curse: Dragon Shifter Romance Collection
If you love alpha romances, dragons, bad boys, and paranormal
shifters who know how to take charge, then you will love Royal
Dragon Curse!

Shifter Secrets: Shifter Romance Collection
Eight sexy beasts that will stop at nothing to claim their mates!

THANK YOU

Thank you for reading my book. Readers like you make an author's world shine. If you've enjoyed this book, or any other books by Lola Gabriel or another author, please don't hesitate to review them on Amazon or Goodreads.

Every single review makes an incredible difference. The reason for this is simple: other readers trust reviews more than professional endorsements. For this reason, indie authors rely on our readers to spread the good word.

Thank you very much! I am giving you a virtual high-five!

Lola Gabriel

ABOUT THE AUTHOR

Lola Gabriel loves reading and writing paranormal romances. Growing up in the Pacific Northwest, she has fond memories of retreating to the woods for long hikes. The towering evergreens, natural waterfalls, and soothing rain often set the scenery for her characters' romantic encounters.

Find out more about Lola Gabriel at SecretWoodsBooks.com

Made in the USA
Lexington, KY
27 May 2019